Three Reasons to Run

Weddings with the Moks, Book 2

Jackie Lau

First edition: August 2024

Print ISBN 978-1-989610-38-1

Editor: Ali Williams

Cover Design: Sarah Kil Creative Studio

Prologue

Leo

Two years earlier...

WHEN I ENTER THE backyard, I feel slightly disoriented, even though I've been here many times before. Someone greets me, and it takes me a moment to respond.

It's weird seeing lots of people in one place and socializing in person. I'm out of practice.

I haven't seen my extended family in well over a year because of COVID-19, but now we've all had our vaccines, and Auntie Gladys is having an outdoor gathering at her house to celebrate her son's engagement. I've never met Carl's fiancée, although they've been together for a few years. Carl and I aren't close, even if we're the same age, so that probably explains it—that and the global pandemic.

I figure I should find my cousin and congratulate him. Get that out of the way.

But then I freeze.

There's a woman standing by the vegetable garden, facing the herbs and tomatoes as she talks to my uncle. Though I can't see her face, I know I've never met her before. I also know that she's very, very beautiful. There's something about the way the sun hits her hair, her arm as she gestures...

She turns, and she's somehow even more gorgeous than I imagined. I wish I could sketch her. I haven't been drawing lately, but suddenly, I'm inspired.

"Hi," she says. "I'm Yvonne. You must be one of Carl's cousins?"

Fuck me.

This is the fiancée. I'd been hoping it was one of her friends.

"I'm Leo."

She holds out her hand, then pulls it back with a laugh that's far too pretty. "I haven't shaken anyone's hand in a long time, but it's still instinctive. Nice to meet you, Leo. Can I get you a drink?"

"No, that's okay." I tug at my collar. "Congratulations. On your engagement." It's amazing that words are actually coming out of my mouth when it feels like my heartbeat has gone haywire.

For the rest of the afternoon, I do my best to make normal conversation with my family and try not to look at Yvonne, but she keeps drawing my gaze. How does the light always hit her features just so, as though she controls it?

Even if she weren't engaged to my cousin, she wouldn't be for me. I know that. In her dress and light cardigan, she's polished and perfectly put together, while I'm rougher around the edges than the other people in my family.

Yet it's the rare moments when she's not so controlled that enchant me. A brief unguarded laugh. The way she tips her head toward the sun when it peeks out from behind the clouds.

I want to muss her up. Set her free.

But my reaction to Yvonne probably has something to do with the fact that I'm not used to meeting new people. I feel like a boy who's never seen anyone pretty before in his life.

Surely by the time they get married, I'll have gotten over this.

Yvonne's Search History

Five Days Before the Wedding

- melatonin dose

- why doesn't melatonin work for me

- how many houseplants is too many

- cold feet before wedding

Four Days Before

- Toronto weather forecast

- how is humidex calculated

- how to hide bags under eyes

Three Days Before

- how to calm racing heart

- percentage of parents who regret having kids

- sibling estrangement

- average age first marriage

Two Days Before

- Runaway Bride movie

- Julia Roberts

- Richard Gere age

- Chicago movie

- does counting sheep really work

- most beautiful houseplants

- best plant stores in Toronto

- why do my partner's snores make me want to punch something

- why do I enjoy power washing videos

- can you power wash a person

- why am I having violent thoughts

- does asmr help you sleep

The Night Before

- is disastrous rehearsal dinner a bad sign

- max dose melatonin

- but seriously why doesn't melatonin work for me

- how do I learn to trust him again

- average price wedding

- Canada US exchange rate

- should I go through with wedding

- cold feet before wedding

- why do I keep googling the same things

- how old is google

- I can't sleep and I'm getting married in ten hours help

Chapter 1

Leo

MY HANDS CLENCH ON the steering wheel as I come to a stop, and a bead of sweat trickles down my temple. Unable to stand it any longer, I loosen my tie. I hate having to dress up like this, and I've done it too many times this summer.

But as I wait for the cop who pulled me over, there's a strange peace in my chest.

Maybe I'll miss it.

For the last few days, my skin has been crawling at the thought of Carl kissing Yvonne in front of a hundred and fifty people. I've had two damn years to get used to the idea—and I *am* used to it.

My body doesn't seem to have gotten the message.

While my tie no longer feels like it's choking me, it's still too much. I loosen it farther, then pull out my license and registration as I wait for the officer. I assume I'm getting a speeding ticket, though I was only going 5 km/h over the limit. I didn't think they'd bother pulling someone over for that.

When the officer approaches, I open the window. He introduces himself, and it soon becomes clear that the speed limit is 40 km/h, not 50 km/h like I thought. I swear that's what the last sign said—it would be the expected speed limit on a road like this—but I won't argue. Nasty things can happen at traffic stops. I don't think that's likely for someone who looks like me, but I still plan to say as little as possible.

15 km/h over the speed limit, but he lowers it to 10. No demerit points, just a small fine, and of course I'd rather do something else with the money, but I can afford it. This is the most trouble I've had with the law. I'm too boring to be a bad boy; I'm just what passes for one in my family.

I glance at the envelope on the seat beside me. Inside the card is a smaller red envelope with more cash than the fine.

"You on your way to a wedding?" the officer asks.

"Yes," I say.

In the distance, I hear an ice cream truck. I've never been one for sweets, but ice cream sounds nice right now: something cool on this hot summer's day. I should be wearing shorts and a T-shirt on an afternoon like this, but instead, I'm in a suit.

"Have a nice day," he says before walking away.

I take the car out of park, then drive down the street, careful not to exceed 40 km/h. There's no way I'm getting to the church in time. When I left my apartment, I didn't give myself much of a time cushion because I didn't want to arrive early. Google Maps said twenty-five minutes; I gave myself thirty.

I pull into a plaza and send a text to Max, telling him that I got a speeding ticket and won't make it for the ceremony. I don't want to sneak in the back while bride is walking down the aisle.

The bride.

I wonder what she looks like today, how the light streaming through the stained-glass windows will hit her. The last wedding I attended was on a rainy day, but of course it's not rainy for Yvonne and Carl, the lucky bastard. I'm sure she'll be absolutely stunning.

The thought causes a terrible pain in my stomach, and I lean over the steering wheel. I know it's ridiculous to feel this way, but I've never been the smart one in the family. All through school, I had to deal with teachers who'd taught my older brothers and were clearly disappointed in me. Max and Evan were great students; I wasn't. The disappointment of my parents, however, was harder to bear, yet I still didn't do what they wanted.

And now, I'm stupid enough to have a crush on my cousin's fiancée. Who, in just a few short minutes, will be his wife. They'll recite their vows, seal it with a kiss, and celebrate in front of family and friends before going on a honeymoon and starting their life together.

I can't stand it.

I feel uncomfortable in my suit. Uncomfortable in my skin. I consider not going to the church at all, just the reception, but I should be there for family pictures.

With a sigh, I back out of the parking spot and continue to the church, my pulse speeding up as I approach. I wish my body would calm the fuck down. I could blame it on being pulled over, but I can't lie to myself, not when I keep picturing her face.

Foolish.

Tonight, Jon will probably make some comment about how weddings are a great place to pick up, and I'll respond with a grunt. I won't join my younger brother as he flirts his way around the room.

I haven't been on a date or slept with anyone since I met Yvonne Siu. I've attempted to interest myself in another woman, but no matter how hard I try, I can't. With the limited socializing I did at the beginning of the pandemic, that means it's been almost four years for me, a fact that I certainly haven't told Jon—or anyone else, for that matter.

It's not like I planned to be faithful to someone I know I can't have; it just happened.

Tomorrow, when I draw a mock-up for the fantasy cover I'm supposed to be working on, the heroine will probably end up looking like Yvonne. I'll curse myself and have to start over.

I never let myself draw her, but occasionally, I do it by accident.

I sigh again and turn on the radio—there's no Bluetooth in my ancient Honda Civic—but every song and commercial annoys me, and I switch it off a few minutes later. It's not much farther anyway. I figure I'll park my car and sit there until I see dresses and suits emerging from the church. People smiling and laughing, happy about the marriage like I ought to be.

But when I turn into the church lot, somebody's already leaving: there's a flash of white skirts hurrying down the steps. I hit the brakes.

Is Yvonne running away from her wedding?

Chapter 2

Yvonne

It started with Francine.

In her tall gray pot, Francine is the picture of elegance. When I bought her five years ago—shortly before I met Carl—I never would have imagined that one day, she'd have me running back up the aisle on my wedding day.

Now, I wasn't actually thinking about her when I bolted, but it was Francine who first made me wonder if I could have more.

You see, back in April, she did something concerning.

She bloomed.

It was the first time she'd flowered. Despite the lovely scent, I wasn't happy; I'd heard that a flowering snake plant could be a sign it's under stress.

"Why are you so worried about a stupid plant?" Carl asked.

When we'd started dating, he seemed to think my love of houseplants was cute. Later, he merely tolerated them...until he called Francine "stupid."

That was the first time I wondered if we shouldn't get married. It was a fleeting thought that caught me by surprise. We'd been together for a while. It was the sensible next step in my life, getting married before my thirtieth birthday, and it wasn't like I could expect him to share my hobbies. Besides, canceling a wedding would be a huge headache, and there were lots of deposits that we wouldn't get back.

As I step into the parking lot, I let out an unhinged laugh.

It definitely would have been easier than—*oh shit.*

I'm momentarily confused when my ass hits the pavement and my feet fly up. But as my bouquet sails through the air, I realize what happened.

I wasn't paying attention to my surroundings and ran straight into a car. I swear it wasn't here three seconds ago.

The driver opens the door a crack, but he can't open it any farther without hitting me. "Are you okay?"

I look up and see Leo, one of Carl's cousins.

Normally, I'd paste on a smile and assure the other person that I'm fine, just fine, but I'm tired of lying, and given the situation, I don't think he'd believe me.

I push myself up to standing. "I've been better"—another unhinged laugh—"but at least nothing's twisted or broken."

When I fled, a part of me thought that I might go back in five minutes, that after making a scene for the first time in my life, I'd realize I wasn't cut out for such things and accept my fate. I went to the church basement, where Carl's aunt, of all people, found me. Lynne didn't march me back upstairs. No, she told me not to get married if I didn't want to, and she gave me her car keys.

I glance at the keys in my hand. Lynne's Toyota is parked in the back corner of the lot. That's how I plan to make my escape, but should I be driving in this condition? I'm a frantic mess. My heart is hammering a million beats a minute and I'm hopped up on adrenaline. I literally just collided with a car that wasn't moving. I don't want to wait for a cab or an Uber, though.

I grab my bouquet—it seems wrong to abandon it, even if I'm not getting married—and before I know what I'm doing, I hurry to the passenger's side of Leo's car.

"Get me out of here," I say as I hop in.

He looks at me for a split second before he turns the car around and heads to the road, while I'm thinking everything and nothing all at once. My thoughts are bouncing together and I can't keep anything straight.

The wedding started on the half hour because it's supposed to be good luck, since the hands on the clock are moving upward. I didn't know that until I started planning this day two years ago. There's so much I've recently learned about weddings that I didn't know before, and it was all for nothing.

Oh my God, what have I done?

Then I grin.

Oh my God, I did it!

I don't have to worry about my future with Carl. We don't need to have more conversations about whether I should quit work when we have kids, and where we're going to move when we have kids...or why he can't put his dirty laundry in the hamper.

I'm free!

My phone buzzes in the small beaded purse on my lap. I take it out and see a text from Erin, my cousin and one of my bridesmaids. I've barely read it when I get another message, this one from Val. I was the maid of honor at her wedding four years ago—a beautiful and lavish affair. When I confessed to her that I was having doubts, she pursed her lips and said I was just overwhelmed with all the planning.

ERIN: Where are you?? It's chaos here.

VAL: I thought you decided to go through with it.

SHAUNA: are you ok?????

JESS: You can come back. It's not too late.

Overwhelmed by the messages from the bridal party, I shove my phone back into my purse as guilt gnaws at me. I've made such a mess. I'm usually the one quietly cleaning up messes, managing other people's feelings.

But here I am, running from my own wedding!

I feel drunk, but I haven't had a drop of alcohol today.

"Where do you want to go?"

The voice startles me, which is silly. Of course the man who's driving me away from my wedding would speak. In fact, it's surprising he took so long to ask that question.

I don't know how to answer, but I feel like I owe him a bit of an explanation. "I couldn't go through with it."

"So I gathered."

Leo is Lynne's son, which is reassuring, since Lynne was so kind to me earlier. I grip her keys as I examine Leo. He's wearing a dark suit and a light blue shirt, the top button undone. His tie hangs loose around his neck. He doesn't look much like Carl. Leo Mok is stockier, and he has slightly darker skin and shaves his head. He's not smiling—come to think of it, I'm not sure I've ever seen him smile—but of course he wouldn't be smiling when a runaway bride has forced herself into his car.

"When I came out of the church," I say, "you were right there. You were late to the wedding."

"Yes."

That's all. A one-word answer.

The silence in the car feels stifling.

"Traffic?" I ask.

"I got my first speeding ticket." He pauses. "Don't worry. I'm not a careless driver. You're safe with me."

I'm sure he's just talking about his driving, but it feels like more than that.

When we're at a stoplight, he pulls off his tie and tosses it on the backseat before returning his hand to the wheel. I get the feeling that Leo, unlike Carl, is uncomfortable in a suit and rarely wears one.

My phone begins vibrating incessantly. I take it out of my purse, not surprised to see a call from my mother. I don't answer, just let it go to voicemail, but the vibrating restarts a few seconds later. This time, my fiancé's name appears on the display. I don't answer his call, either, but I can hear his voice in my head.

What the fuck, Yvonne?

In general, I've lived my life so that people don't say such things to me. And now, with one single action, I've blown that all up.

What the fuck, indeed.

I was too chickenshit to call off the wedding, but by the time I started walking down the aisle, I found I just...couldn't. It wasn't so much a decision as a necessity. I was overwhelmed by my feelings, which is rare for me. It didn't feel like the happiest day of my life; it felt like my life was over. The articles I read while I was getting my hair done—about all the women who are happier after a divorce—rang loudly in my head. Why wait until after a divorce to be happier? Why not avoid marriage instead?

Another phone call. It's my mother.

Okay, maybe I won't be happier without Carl, because now I have to deal with the fallout of my actions. All that wasted money.

And Carl and I live together! Where am I going to go? I don't even know where I'll sleep tonight. My parents' house isn't an option. My mom will go on and on about what people must be thinking. My dad will be furious, yelling about the shame I've brought to my family.

What have I done?

I can't get enough air into my lungs, and my head doesn't feel right. I whip off the veil and throw it—as well as my bouquet—in the back with Leo's tie, but it's not enough.

God, I wish I could get out of this dress. I don't even like it. I mean, I don't hate it, but it's not what I'd have chosen if it had just been up to me. I couldn't go against what my mother wanted, though. I was beaten down, after hours and hours of looking at dresses, and I just wanted it all to be over, so I went along with her choice, like I've gone along with so many things in the past.

But not today.

Oh God. How am I going to handle this?

I put my head in my hands, and when Leo stops at a red light, I feel even worse. I think I'm hyperventilating, and why is my mother calling me *again*? Hasn't she gotten the message that I'm not going to pick up?

My phone keeps buzzing. More messages from relatives and bridesmaids.

I ignore them and open the window. But the fresh air doesn't help because it's hotter than the air-conditioned car, so I close the window, then realize Leo has put on the parking brake.

Huh. We're at a park.

He comes around to the passenger's side and helps me out—and it's a good thing he does. I'm a little unsteady on my feet. He leads me over to a tree and puts a bottle of water in my hands.

"Sorry, it's not cold," he says.

I drink half the bottle before I remember my manners.

"Thank you." I attempt a smile. He didn't have to drive me away from the church, to…wherever we are right now. I should be gracious.

"Congratulations!" someone shouts.

I look up and see two young women on the path nearby. I guess they've gotten the wrong impression because I'm in a princess wedding dress and Leo is in a suit.

I stiffen. "No, we're not…he's not my husband."

Husband. The word sticks in my throat.

I don't want a husband. Any husband.

I always imagined I'd get married, from the time I was a little girl, but now, the thought hits me with shocking clarity. I don't want a husband, and it's not because I want a wife instead. I'm attracted to men, romantically and sexually, but I don't want the hassle.

Because that's how I see a husband: a hassle.

And I deserve better.

For the first time since I left the church, tears come to my eyes—and I'm sure it's obvious they aren't tears of joy. I've destroyed the life that I meticulously planned. The life that would make my parents happy.

The young women approach us, concerned.

"Are you okay?" one of them asks. "Do you need me to call someone for you?"

The other eyes Leo suspiciously.

"He's a family friend," I say quickly. "I left my fiancé at the altar, but it's fine. I'll be fine." I'm not convinced of that, but I don't want to make these strangers worry.

After they walk away, I exhale slowly and tell myself to take deep breaths. I do feel a bit better after drinking water, though I'm hungry.

And then I hear it. An ice cream truck.

"Do you want ice cream?" Leo asks.

I nod. Soft ice cream, cold and sweet—that sounds amazing. Nowhere near as fancy as what I was supposed to eat later, but I don't care.

I follow him to the truck, and we wait behind a family. A girl, who's about seven, eyes me curiously but doesn't say anything. I suppose a bride waiting in line at an ice cream truck isn't an everyday sight. I feel a bit like Giselle in *Enchanted*.

Leo gets two cones of chocolate vanilla twist and pays before I can protest. We step onto the grass and lick our ice cream, and somehow, this is the greatest ice cream I've ever had. I know, objectively, that isn't true, but it's exactly what I need right now. I haven't eaten much today. In fact, I haven't eaten much in the past three months, just so I could fit into this stupid dress.

When I glance at Leo, his tongue darts out at the swirls of ice cream, and all of a sudden, I remember telling Lynne that my fiancé isn't great in bed.

Why am I thinking about such things?

Weird.

"You, uh..." Leo gestures to my skirts.

Oops. I spilled chocolate ice cream on my dress. I cringe before reminding myself that it's okay. What do I need this dress for anyway? Sure, it cost a shitload of money, but there was probably already a stain or rip on the back from when I fell, and it's not like I'm going to wear it again.

I finish my ice cream before it all melts in the hot sun, then wipe my hands on my dress just because I can. I feel wild and out of control and unlike myself.

I feel high on life...and I also want to curl up in a ball and cry.

"Where would you like to go now?" Leo asks.

"I can't impose on you any longer—"

"My only plan for today was the wedding. It's not like I have anything else to do. I'll drive you home."

"I live with Carl," I say miserably.

"Then let's get your stuff out of there."

Chapter 3

Leo

I PULL OUT OF the parking lot and immediately see a sign that says 50 km/h.

I don't go above 48 km/h.

And I don't look over at Yvonne, even though my eyes have been drawn in that direction for the past hour. I need to focus on the road. On doing what I can do for her.

I don't ask *why* she ran. I figure if she wants to tell me, she will, and I don't want to etch more pain on her face.

She directs me to her building and asks for my license plate number so she can register my car for visitor parking. Despite the situation, she doesn't forget that detail.

As we take the elevator to the fourth floor, my hands clench. What if Carl's here? I doubt he will be, but you never know. He could have arrived by now if he wanted.

After she clumsily fits the key in the lock, her phone buzzes again. It's been blowing up for the past hour, and she hasn't typed a text or answered a call...or put it on silent.

"I'm sure your family is concerned about you," I say, feeling out of my depth. "And your bridesmaids. Maybe you should let them know where you are?"

"I can't handle my parents right now. I just *can't*. But..."

She types a quick text before stuffing her phone back in her tiny purse.

Once we're inside the apartment—which is thankfully free of Carl—Yvonne pulls a suitcase out of the closet and heads to the bedroom. I stay in the main living area, feeling useless, but it seems like an invasion of privacy to watch her pack. Sure, I might have transported her away from her wedding, but I don't know her that well.

I know the light always hits her in a dazzling way that makes me itch to sketch her.

I know she has a degree, unlike me, and works as a business analyst in the healthcare sector. I'm not sure exactly what that entails, but I bet she's good at it.

I know she's a capable person who gets things done.

I also know she's not the kind of person who tries to make waves or draw attention to herself, even if *my* attention is always drawn to her.

She's not flighty. She's not the woman you'd expected to leave her fiancé at the altar.

What the hell did Carl do to her?

I've long wanted to see her when she's not so put together, but this isn't what I imagined; I didn't want to see her in distress, even if a silly part of me is glad she didn't marry my cousin.

Yvonne exits her bedroom with the suitcase and a couple of overflowing tote bags. She's changed into jeans and a simple tank top, but she still has her glamorous makeup and updo.

"Anything else you need?" I ask. My car won't fit all of her belongings, but it can handle a little more than what she's packed so far.

Her gaze darts toward the other side of the room, where there are several plants.

"I can't take them all," she says mournfully. "I'll have to come back another day. But I can't leave Francine." She walks over to a pot containing a cluster of near-vertical leaves, and for the first time since she got in my car, she truly smiles.

"Do you have something we could put Francine in?" I ask. I don't want her to fall over on the drive to…wherever we're going next.

Yvonne gives me an odd look before saying, "Yes, of course."

She grabs a cardboard box, and with care, she sets the pot inside.

I reach for the handle of the suitcase. "Let's go."

"Wait!"

She returns to the bedroom and comes out with her wedding dress.

I raise an eyebrow.

"I'm not leaving it here," she says. "I'm going to destroy it properly."

I don't ask what that means.

"Carl hated Francine," Yvonne says when we're back in the car. She told me to head east, but I don't know exactly where we're going.

"She's a plant," I say. I hope that's not insulting—I don't mean it to be. Actually, I think it's rather sweet that she didn't want to leave Francine behind.

But Francine is a plant. That's a fact. How could my cousin hate a houseplant?

"He called her stupid when I worried that she wasn't healthy," Yvonne explains. "Then there was the cat-sitting incident. Carl's friend and his wife were going on vacation, and Carl said we'd cat sit for them, without consulting me. If he had, he would have known that snake plants like Francine are toxic for cats."

Yeah, that doesn't sound like a good combination.

"I told him we couldn't do it," Yvonne says, "and he told me I was being ridiculous and we should get rid of her, even though I've had her for five years. I suppose we could have put her in the bedroom and kept the cat out of there, but what if the cat destroyed the other plants? Besides, I would have done all the work."

This doesn't surprise me. Carl, the youngest and only boy out of three kids, was always rather spoiled. I imagine he'd consider himself too important to care for someone else's pet. He might have agreed to it, but he'd make his fiancée do the actual work.

I don't say that.

"Where are we going?" I ask.

"Dinner," she says. "I know it's early, but I'm starving. My treat, since you've been so helpful today and you paid for ice cream. What would you like? We're near a burger joint, but if you want something else—"

"No, that's good."

Ten minutes later, we're in a booth at a restaurant that looks like it hasn't been renovated in decades. I shed my suit jacket and rolled up my sleeves, since there isn't much in the way of air conditioning.

The conversation—or lack thereof—is a little awkward. Staying quiet doesn't usually feel awkward to me, but it does now, even if I'm distracted by how my dining companion looks in the harsh lighting. It highlights her angles in a captivating way.

When the server sets our plates, both heaped with a generous portion of fries, on the table, Yvonne douses hers in vinegar and eagerly digs in.

She groans after finishing her first fry. "The fries here are my favorite."

Maybe they are amazing, but I've yet to try one because I'm staring at her and wondering how the hell Carl allowed this to happen. Not that he should have run after her and prevented her from leaving the church—that's not what I mean.

No, how did he not do everything in his power to keep her happy?

If she were my—

I dismiss that thought as quickly as possible.

I'm being a friend to her today. That's what she needs.

"So, Leo," she says. "You're a drafter, right?"

"Yes." I'm not sure what else to say. I'm having trouble wrapping my mind around the fact that, after the day she's had, she wants to make small talk. But maybe she wants to take her mind off it, so I do my best. "I work for a small engineering firm. I spend most of my day using AutoCAD."

When I finished high school, I got a manual labor job. At first, it was a great change from school. But then I started to have back problems, and I began wondering if this was really the kind of work I wanted to do for decades.

Drafting was Max's idea—he's an engineer, and he thought I'd be good at it. It had never occurred to me. Yes, it involved going back to school, but I got a diploma in two years and it wasn't so bad. It doesn't bring me any great sense of fulfillment, but it's a steady paycheck, the hours are decent, and I don't have lots of annoying meetings. Then afterward, I go to the gym.

"I wish I was working on Monday," Yvonne says. "Losing myself in spreadsheets sounds good right about now. But I took some time off for the wedding, so I'm not returning until Wednesday."

I consider asking about the honeymoon, but I keep my mouth shut in case that's a sensitive topic right now.

As it turns out, it's the next thing she brings up.

"The honeymoon isn't for several weeks. No flying involved, just driving to the Finger Lakes, and it shouldn't be a problem to cancel the accommodation with this much notice." She sighs and bites into her burger.

Not sure what to say, I grunt and remove the pickles before biting into my own burger.

She was right: this place is really good.

Juice dribbles down my chin, and I wipe it off with a napkin before putting some vinegar on my fries.

"You like vinegar on fries, too!" she says. "Carl thought it was silly. He's a ketchup guy." She slides her hand across the table. "Thank you, Leo, for everything. You didn't have to, but I really appreciate it."

Slightly uncomfortable with her thanks, with the sincerity in her voice, I grunt and reach for another fry. Then I notice that her gaze has dropped from my face to the pickles on my plate.

"Help yourself," I say.

She smiles and sticks one in her mouth, and once again, I find myself wondering how Carl ever allowed this to happen. Her shiny makeup contrasts with her casual clothes and the pickles she's consuming. She seems to genuinely be enjoying herself now, and she's not trying to maintain her polish. She's managed to relax a little.

When we finish, I allow her to pay—I know she would fight me if I didn't let her—and return to my car. I wish I had something nicer than this beat-up vehicle for her. At least the air conditioning still works.

"Where to?" I ask.

Her face falls. "I'm not sure where I'm going to spend the night."

I don't offer my own place. First of all, it would give me ideas that I ought to keep out of my head. Second of all, I have a studio apartment. Not only is there just one bed; there's just one room.

Nor do I suggest she stay with her parents or one of her bridesmaids. I'm sure those options would have occurred to her, and she seems to be avoiding them. I'm annoyed that this woman doesn't really have anyone in her corner.

Finally, she lifts her chin. "I'll go to my sister's. It's about twenty minutes away."

I don't recall her mentioning a sister before, but rather than asking questions, I back out of the parking spot. She gives me directions to a residential neighborhood in Scarborough.

"You can park on the street," she says. "My sister lives in a basement apartment. At least, I assume she still lives here."

Huh.

We get out of the car. I take Yvonne's suitcase out of the trunk while she grabs the bags and the wedding dress. When I reach for the plant, which is on the floor behind the passenger's seat, she places a hand on my arm.

I freeze.

She immediately steps back. "Sorry, sorry!"

I didn't freeze because the touch was unwelcome; no, it was just consuming so much of my attention that I couldn't even move.

I don't tell her that, of course.

"It's fine," I say gruffly.

"No, no, you've been so helpful today, and I'm going to ask two more favors of you. First, can you return your mom's car keys?" She removes them from her purse. "And please, thank her for me again."

I pocket the keys and frown. "Why did you have them?"

"She gave them to me, to help me escape, but then I ran into you."

I barely have time to process that before she speaks again.

"Second." Her gaze slides toward the plant. "Can you look after Francine for a little while? Tracey has two cats, and I don't want to show up with a plant that's toxic for her pets. Assuming you don't have any cats or dogs, that is."

"No pets. I can do it." I don't the first thing about plants, but how hard can it be?

"Great! What's your number? Snake plants are pretty easy to care for, but I'll text you the instructions."

"Doesn't she just need sunlight and water?"

"She *does* need sunlight and water, but you have to know how much."

I nod. "I can manage that."

After I dictate my number, she heads to a door at the side of the house, and I follow with her suitcase.

"Tracey doesn't know I'm coming," she says before knocking.

We wait for someone to answer. Just when I'm about to suggest she send a text, the door swings open. It's a young white man, and for a split second, I remember what Yvonne said earlier. *I assume she still lives here.*

Then he says, "Hi, Yvonne."

Ah. This must be her sister's partner.

A moment later, an Asian woman appears. Her facial features bear a striking resemblance to Yvonne's, and they're the same height and have similar builds, except...

Yvonne's sister is heavily pregnant. She looks like she could go into labor at any moment.

"I thought you were getting married today?" Her gaze skims over Yvonne, bags and dress in hand, before widening. "Did you not—"

"You're *pregnant?*"

Chapter 4

Yvonne

Leo is probably wondering what the fuck is wrong with my family.

Why didn't I know my sister is having a baby?

Why wasn't she at the wedding that didn't happen?

But before I can figure out what to tell him, Tracey embraces me, her pregnant belly hitting me before her arms come around my shoulders.

When I step back, I glance over my shoulder, and Leo gives me a silent nod. He disappears before I can thank him again.

"Who's that?" Tracey asks, waggling her eyebrows.

"You think I didn't marry Carl because of another man?" I give her a look. "It's Carl's cousin. He just drove me to pick up my stuff."

"So why didn't you get married?"

"I didn't want to. I *couldn't*. The minister said, 'We are gathered here today'...and I ran."

Tracey laughs. "I can't believe you did that. I'm proud of you."

Yeah, I came to the one person who'd be proud of me. My big sister. Leaving someone at the altar sounds like the sort of thing she'd do.

Yet she's the one who's married, not me. She and Rob got married a year ago, with only two witnesses in attendance. I wasn't there; our parents certainly weren't there.

We might not be close, but I did invite her to my wedding. In fact, I pleaded with her to come. I told her that she didn't have to be in the wedding party and I'd seat her far away from our mom and dad.

But she still said no.

Now, I wonder if it's because of the pregnancy. If she weren't so far along, maybe she could hide it, but she's clearly close to her due date.

Tracey is three years older than me, which surprises some people. I give off responsible eldest daughter vibes, I guess, and she—well, she was a bit of a troubled teen. Drinking, drugs, skipping class. The sort of things that, as a daughter of Asian immigrants, you're definitely *not* supposed to do.

I, meanwhile, saw my parents struggle with her, and I decided to do whatever I could so they wouldn't worry about me.

I always wished we were closer, in part so I could convince her to change—though I don't want her to change now. Back in the day, she'd occasionally make snarky comments about me being a goody two-shoes, but mostly, she just ignored me. Whenever she was home, her time was taken up having arguments with our parents, but she stopped talking to them when she dropped out of university after one semester.

"You need a drink," she declares. "I won't join you, of course, but I can make you something. What do you want?"

"A shot," I say, remembering the time she dared me to do a shot when I was sixteen.

I refused, naturally.

"A shot of what?" she asks.

"Whatever you have." I don't plan to get drunk, but a little alcohol sounds good.

Something that burns.

She pours me a shot of vodka, and we sit at the small table in the corner of the main room. I haven't been here in two years. There's a suitcase—not mine—by the couch. I assume it's her packed bag to take to the hospital, whenever the time comes. Rob has disappeared. I guess he's decided to give us space.

"What did that fucker do?" Tracey asks.

"General assholery," I reply.

She chuckles without mirth. "Sounds fancy when you say it like that. He didn't, I don't know, sleep with your maid of honor after the rehearsal dinner? Snort coke off your cousin's chest?"

"Which cousin are you thinking of?"

"I don't know, but isn't that the sort of thing finance bros do?"

I tense, but I don't tell her what I discovered three months ago.

Instead, I reach for the shot and toss it back.

She whoops.

"Still working at the same hair salon?" I ask.

She rolls her eyes as she pours me another drink. "Seriously? Tell me what he did to make my perfect little sister run."

I tense again, despite the vodka coursing through my veins. That dig about me being perfect...it reminds me of our strained relationship.

And I can't tell her everything. It's too mortifying.

"As I was walking down the aisle," I say, "it felt like the biggest mistake of my life. We'd have kids, and I'd do all the work, and..."

I glance around the room. There's a pile of baby clothes on an end table. Did Tracey have a baby shower? Did she ever consider inviting me?

"Boy or girl?" I ask instead.

"Boy," she says.

"Carl's the only son. He has two older sisters, who both got married this summer, too. Well, I suppose he didn't end up getting married after all..."

In the silence that follows, I regard my sister, who's wearing a gray T-shirt over her bump. Unlike usual, her hair isn't dyed. It's dark, like mine, and I think that cut is called a contoured bob—I saw it in a listicle the other day.

"How's the pregnancy?" I ask.

"My feet are swollen as fuck now," she says, "and I turned on the air conditioning in early May, but I know I've been lucky."

Rob appears with a platter of oatmeal cookies and a glass that looks like it's filled with iced tea. He sets the drink in front of Tracey, then rubs her shoulders. I feel like I'm interfering in a nice domestic moment.

"Did you make the cookies?" I ask.

"Yes," Rob says.

His conversational skills remind me of Leo, and I bite back a smile as I down more vodka. This shot burns more than the first one, and I start coughing. Wordlessly, Tracey slides over her iced tea, and I drink half of it while Rob gets her another.

I debate having a cookie. I never eat more than one "treat" in a day, and I've already had ice cream, but fuck that. I don't need to fit into a wedding dress anymore, and it's been a hard day.

Tracey and I each reach for the same cookie, but she lets me have it and takes another. Maybe it's that small gesture—well, to be honest, it's probably the shots—but I say, "Why didn't you tell me about the pregnancy?"

Rob and Tracey look at each other, and it seems like they're having a whole conversation without speaking. I feel a *whoosh* of jealousy.

Carl and I didn't have that connection, and I was the one who did everything right, whereas Tracey—

I shut down that poisonous thought. It's not that I don't think my sister deserves happiness, but some small part of me can't help it.

"It's okay," I say quickly. "It's fine. It's your choice. I just...would have liked to know, and I promise I wouldn't have told anyone."

Tracey simply nods. She doesn't give me a snarky response, but after that, our conversation feels forced.

Later, as I try to make myself comfortable on the couch, I realize that my initial plan to stay here for a few days won't work, even if Tracey grudgingly lets me. I need to get out of here as soon as possible so my sister can prepare for the birth of her first child in peace.

I wake up sore from spending seven hours on a couch, but at least I slept, unlike the night before. It seems like a sign that I did the right thing.

Or it's just a sign that I was exhausted to the bone.

I can't make out what Tracey and Rob are saying, but I can hear the rumble of conversation in the bedroom...and then a soft meow.

Burrito rubs up against my leg. I pat his head.

Blade, on the other hand, eyes me suspiciously from beneath the TV stand.

I hope Tracey hasn't been changing the litter—I'm pretty sure you're not supposed to do that when you're pregnant. And how will the cats react to the baby? My instinct is to talk to her about it, make sure she's being responsible, but she can google things herself and has a partner who does chores. Surely, she has this in hand, and I know she'll snap if I suggest otherwise.

Our relationship bears so many scars from the past.

If I hadn't come here yesterday, when she would have told me her news? Would I have received a picture of her holding a newborn at the hospital? Or would she have waited even longer? How much of a relationship will she allow me to have with the baby?

In recent weeks, the thought of having my own kids has made me freak out, but it's not like babies in general freak me out. I look forward to meeting my nephew.

The apartment isn't much different from the last time I was here. There's limited natural light, it being a basement apartment and all, but still enough that without turning on a lamp, I can see that the single plant—a cast iron plant—doesn't look the healthiest. It does well in low light and it's not dangerous for cats, though, so it's a good option for Tracey.

That reminds me of Francine. I pick up my phone, ignore the texts I've gotten overnight, and pull up Leo's contact info. I still need to send him instructions. Maybe he'll think I'm just a weird plant lady, but I can't worry too much about what impression he has of me after yesterday.

Before I can send a text, my phone vibrates in my hand.

Carl.

I'm tempted to send it to voicemail again, but then the guilt sets in. I do feel like I owe him *something*.

"Hi." I lean back on the couch where I spent the night.

"That's all you have to say to me?"

The sound of his voice makes me tense.

"What the hell, Yvonne? Do you know how humiliating that was? How could you do this to me?"

"I'm sorry," I reply instinctively. "You didn't deserve that." Then, because I'm a different person than I was before, I say, "I should have ended things earlier. I was just...scared. I thought I could still go through with it, but it turns out, I couldn't."

"I've been good to you."

I almost snort.

"I apologized for what happened," he says. "I promised it wouldn't happen again. What more did you want from me?"

I don't respond.

"Is there someone else?" he demands. "You think you can do better?"

"There's no one else." I ignore the second question. I'm not sure I can do better in a relationship, but being single is better than a life with Carl.

"You have to pay back my parents for all the money they wasted."

I'll have to pay back my own parents, too. I have savings—savings I planned to use as a down payment to buy a house with Carl—but this will obliterate them, and it still won't be enough. I also need to get an apartment in the ridiculous Toronto rental market. The place where I was living is in his name only. I moved in with him. I have no claim on it, officially.

"If you don't have the rest of your stuff out by Friday," he says, "I'm tossing it."

"I'll come tomorrow or Tuesday while you're at work." I don't have a vehicle, but I'll figure it out somehow.

"I don't think you understand the mess I had to deal with yesterday."

God forbid Carl had to *deal with* something for once in his personal life. I was the one who made things run smoothly.

But I do feel bad for him. Just a teeny-tiny bit.

Then I realize he hasn't said a single word about being heartbroken. No, he's talking about the hassle, the humiliation, the wasted money, but not that. Did I ever mean anything to him?

"Val and Jess are pissed, too," he says. "Think of all the work they did for the wedding."

"More than you did." The words pop out of my mouth.

"You're not who I thought you were," Carl mutters. "Maybe it's good we didn't get married."

"You see? I was right to run away."

But I wish I hadn't forgiven him after he cheated on me.

Chapter 5

Leo

As I SIP MY morning coffee, I check my phone. I've got a series of texts from Yvonne, telling me how to care for Francine.

I send her a quick reply. *Got it.*

One thing I've never been great at: communication. Whether I'm speaking or writing, nobody would ever think of me as a great communicator, which was clear from some of the comments I received on my report cards.

But I can get things done, and I *will* take care of this plant.

I move Francine to a place that I think has the right amount of light, according to Yvonne's instructions. Then I glance at the wilted bouquet and veil sitting on my counter, the other signs of the hours I spent with Yvonne yesterday. I guess I'll ask her about the veil later—she probably has enough to handle today—and discard the flowers when I head out this afternoon.

For now, however, it's time to get started on that cover.

After a couple hours of drawing—somehow, I manage not to make the heroine look like Yvonne—I head to my childhood home in North York. My parents are sitting on the porch when I arrive.

Appearance-wise, I take after my dad more than any of my brothers do. We have similar builds, and we both started going bald early. As a result, I began shaving my head at twenty-five, and when barbershops were closed due to the pandemic, my hairstyle didn't have to change at all. I took care of it every two weeks with my clippers.

But temperament? We share no similarities there.

"Leo." My dad grins as I walk up the steps. He gets to his feet and pulls me in for a hug. Asian fathers might not be renowned for their affection, but mine is a hugger. "Didn't see you yesterday, but I assume you heard what happened?"

"Yeah, that's why I'm here." I take the keys out of my pocket.

My mom's eyebrows rise.

"Yvonne was leaving as I pulled up," I say. "So I drove her. She said to, uh, thank you for giving her the keys, but I don't think she was in the best state to drive herself."

Mom nods. "Where is she now? They lived together, yes?"

Should I say she's at her sister's? And *is* she still at her sister's? Their relationship is a mystery to me. I suppose Yvonne wouldn't want Carl's parents to know, and since my dad is Carl's dad's brother...

You see? Communicating is complicated.

"She's safe," I grunt.

Inside the house, the landline rings. Nobody moves to answer it.

"It's Gladys," Mom says. Carl's mother and my mother have never gotten along.

"I assume she wasn't happy yesterday," I say.

Mom, still seated on the patio chair, lets out an uncharacteristic snort-laugh.

"How about Carl?" I ask.

"His groomsmen took him out and got him drunk, I think," Dad says.

They probably told him that Yvonne was a bitch and he was too good for her.

That pisses me off.

My parents don't ask many questions about what she and I did together. My mom and dad are far from the world's nosiest people, but I still expected them to make more inquiries. Instead, they seem to want to give Yvonne her privacy.

I do want to make one thing clear, though. "We weren't...there's nothing between us. I only drove her because I showed up at the right time."

"I never thought there was." Dad looks at me as if to say, *But the fact that you're bringing it up is suspicious.*

Jesus.

You see? This is why communicating is so complicated.

Mom gives him a look I can't interpret before standing up. I follow her into the house, where she'll undoubtedly get me some food. Even if she didn't know I was coming until I texted this morning, there's no way I can leave without her giving me something.

Things between me and my parents aren't so bad now. When I was seventeen and flat-out refused to apply to university, it was different. They told me I didn't need to go to a top school—it wasn't like I would have gotten in anyway—but surely, I could get in *somewhere.*

They were probably right: there's a good chance one or two universities in the province would have taken me. But the thought of another year in a classroom made me want to claw my eyes out, and it wasn't like there was a subject I wished to study.

"If she needs anything," Mom says now as she reaches for a bag in the pantry, "we can help her, okay? I don't think her parents will, and I'm worried about her."

My eyebrows shoot up. I'm not used to my mother so clearly expressing concern for someone outside of our family. She's usually quiet about such things—some people think she's cold—and not nearly as outgoing as my father.

In some ways, I take after her.

"Okay," I say. "I'll let her know." I shouldn't be thankful to have a good reason to text Yvonne, but I am.

As I head to my car, I can't help wondering what she told my mother. Does Mom know more about what happened with Carl than I do?

And does my cousin deserve a punch in the face?

Chapter 6

Yvonne

I FEEL BETTER AFTER a shower, so when I return to Tracey's couch, I do something I've been putting off: I open up the group chat with my bridesmaids. Before I start typing, I scroll up and look through happy messages about the bachelorette party, messages that don't show the doubts I was experiencing.

> YVONNE: I'm sorry for being off the grid for the past twenty-four hours. I'm at my sister's for now. I'm okay. I should have had the guts to call off the wedding a long time ago, but I didn't...and so I ran. I'm sorry I put you all through those fittings, etc. for nothing. I didn't intend for this to happen.
>
> VAL: I'm glad you're okay, but I think you'll regret this.

The next message I get is from Shauna, but it's not in the group chat. She tells me that she's going to call and I better pick up.

When I see the incoming video call, I answer.

"Yvonne!" Shauna says. "Oh my God. I've been worried sick about you. But you're at Tracey's? You're really okay? I tried to look for you. At first, I couldn't move because I was in shock, but then I walked around the church and the gardens..."

Shauna Tran's chatter makes me smile. I remember all the time we used to spend together in high school.

"Another wedding guest helped me escape." I consider saying more. Once upon a time, I would have told Shauna everything, but as we got older, we merely had catch-up lunches twice a year. That was all. Then I asked her to be my bridesmaid because I missed her and wanted to see her more often, but I haven't told her everything in a long, long time.

Her voice changes. "You know I'm on your side no matter what, right? I'm sure you had a good reason, even if it was impulsive. You can stay here for a few days, if you like. I know you're not close with your sister."

I really need to get out of Tracey's apartment, but I can't intrude on Shauna too much. She lives with her parents.

"Just let me know." She pauses. "You'd tell me if you were in danger, right?"

"I'm not in danger," I assure her. "Carl is pissed, but the most he'd do is destroy my plants." The thought makes me want to cry, but at least Francine is safe.

There's a long silence. I'm not sure how much I want to lean on Shauna. I haven't been the greatest friend to her in the past decade. When we went to different universities, we started to drift apart, which was more my fault than hers.

"Why is Val being such an ass?" she asks.

"A few days ago, I told her that I was having doubts, and she dismissed them. Said I was being silly."

Another silence. I don't feel like repeating what I told Val. Not because I'm unsure of what Shauna's reaction would be...

Okay, maybe that's part of it. A tiny sliver of doubt, despite her reassurances, because of what happened with Val. But also, I just don't feel like getting into it now.

"You can help me figure out what to do with the wedding dress," I say instead.

"It's Halloween in just over two months. You're going as a zombie bride. We'll pour fake blood all over it."

"I can't remember the last time I did anything for Halloween."

"We'll find a party. Leave that to me."

After I get off the phone, I stare into space for a few minutes. Then, all of a sudden, tears start streaming down my face.

How is this my life?

I usually have everything planned out—the spreadsheets I made for the wedding are things of beauty—yet I don't even know where I'm sleeping tonight. I've destroyed all my best-laid plans. Some of the people I called my friends? They're clearly not my friends anymore.

It's fucking terrifying.

But of all those people, Shauna has known me the longest, and she's confident I had good reasons for not wanting to get married.

I did. Three very good reasons, and I write them down in a notes app to remind myself.

First of all, it had become clear that Carl and I had different hopes for the future. His involved kids (that he wouldn't spend much time with) and a dutiful wife who'd put everything he wanted ahead of her own dreams. When he spoke about his vision of the future, it felt like he didn't understand me, not even a little. Why should I tie myself to someone like that?

Second of all, I don't love him. I assume I did love him once, but somewhere along the way, I stopped. Probably even before my third reason happened.

He slept with another woman, and despite his promises, I can't trust him.

How did I not see the signs?

But even without knowing that he cheated, Lynne encouraged me to leave if I didn't want to get married. On one hand, it seems selfish to focus on my personal wants and not think about my (ex) fiancé and family, but it's my life. Shouldn't that at least count for something?

I blow out a breath. I need to look forward and not backward. This is an opportunity to do things that I've never done in adulthood, so I start another list with goals for my new life.

Live alone. I've never lived alone, but after Carl, I find myself craving the experience. My own space, nobody to tell me that I have too many fucking plants. I don't care if it's small. It's going to be mine.

Have great sex.

As soon as I type that one out, I delete it. What if it's just not possible for me?

Try to have great sex.

That sounds wishy-washy, but I'm not confident enough to keep what I first wrote.

It'll need to be sex outside of a relationship, though, because I'm sure as hell not interested in one of those. I've only had sex with boyfriends in the past, but I'm going to try something new. Probably not right away. Sometime in the next year.

Figure out who I am and build the life that I want for myself.

Thanks to Carl, I have a pretty good idea of who I'm not and what I don't want, but who the hell *am* I? I was so focused on what I thought I *should* have that I lost sight of it. I'm going to allow myself to be spontaneous, waste time, and say no even if it'll make things awkward.

Finding a place to stay is my priority, though. I'm not going to find an apartment of my own in the next twenty-four hours, so I need temporary housing until I sort that out.

My phone buzzes.

> LEO: I returned the car keys. My mom says
> to let her know if you need anything.

I barely know Lynne, but I doubt she'd say that if she didn't mean it. After a moment's hesitation, I give her a call.

The phone rings and rings, and just when I think she won't answer...she does.

Chapter 7

Leo

"How was your weekend?" Dinesh asks as we're getting our coffee.

I don't tell him that I got a speeding ticket and spent Saturday with a runaway bride. Fortunately, he doesn't know I was going to a wedding, so he doesn't ask about that.

I share little about my personal life at work, and Dinesh—one of the engineers—isn't the sort to try to badger information out of people. He just asks friendly questions when he sees me, that ever-present smile on his face. I don't mind him.

"Not too bad," I say.

He mentions taking his family up to Wasaga, but he doesn't keep me for long.

"You'll have the drawings done this afternoon?" he says.

I nod and he slaps me on the back before going to his desk.

Coffee in hand, I get to work at my computer. Monday mornings are always a little rough, but I'm having more trouble focusing than usual, and the text I get at ten doesn't help.

YVONNE: I hate to ask, but can you do another favor for me?

LEO: What sort of favor?

YVONNE: I'm staying with your parents...

When I relayed the message from my mom, this wasn't the sort of "help" I imagined. I'm not sure what I expected, to be honest, but it wasn't this.

I mean, I'm glad Yvonne has somewhere to stay, and there's room at my parents' house. But this means I'll see more of her.

> YVONNE: Would you be able to help move the rest of my stuff today? I don't want to ask your mom or dad.

"Fuck me," I mutter, setting down my phone.

My words draw the attention of Pablo. In the Philippines, he was an engineer, but he's working as a drafter here for now. He doesn't ask what's wrong, just returns his gaze to his screen.

It's not that I have a problem with seeing Yvonne again. The problem is that I like it a little too much. The idea of helping her move almost makes me feel—dear God—*excited*, even though I know nothing can happen between us. She was supposed to get married two days ago, for fuck's sake. To my cousin.

Which is actually a good reason not to do this. If Carl sees me helping Yvonne, he'll get the wrong idea.

> YVONNE: I'll meet you at my old apartment? Carl won't be there until 7.

Well, I guess I don't have that excuse anymore, and I don't know who else she has to ask. Clearly, she doesn't want to trouble her pregnant sister.

I tell her that I can help, then return to my work.

"Thank you," Yvonne says.

I'm uncomfortable with her gratitude. I'm generally uncomfortable with such things, but it's worse with her because this doesn't feel like a selfless act, not when I get to see the sunlight hit her face.

"It's no problem," I grunt as we head into the high-rise.

She's dressed in shorts and a tank top. She looks good—she always does—but there are dark circles under her eyes, and I wish I could brush them away.

As promised, Carl isn't in the apartment. In fact, it looks like she was here alone for a few hours before I arrived—her stuff is packed and neatly arranged by the door. Most of her plants are in two cardboard boxes without lids, and the largest plant is in a box by itself.

Once we cram everything into the trunk and backseat of my car, I start driving in the direction of my childhood home.

"I would have asked you to bring Francine," Yvonne says, "but you came straight from work, right? Next time you visit your parents, you can bring her. How's she doing?"

"She's fine," I say, and we lapse into silence as I fight my way through Toronto traffic.

"If I'm asking too much of you—"

"I can take care of a goddamn plant."

My hands tighten on the steering wheel as familiar feelings of inadequacy rise up, even though I'm sure that's not how she means it. She's just afraid of being an inconvenience, and she didn't deserve my harsh tone.

"If I didn't want to do it," I say, "I would have said no."

"But it can be hard to say no. I know that."

I wonder what's on her mind right now. Did she consider saying no when Carl proposed? (I don't know much about the proposal, but I do know that he was the one who asked.) When she was planning that wedding, how many times did she want to say no but pasted on a smile instead?

"I think it's harder for you than it is for me," I say.

"True. I know it's partly because women are expected to be more accommodating and polite, but I need to stop doing that if it means making myself small."

"Running away from your own wedding was a good start."

She laughs. I'm not a very funny guy, but I think she's desperate to find laughter in any place she can right now.

"You think I made the right choice?" she asks.

I'm glad I'm driving and can't be expected to look at her during this conversation.

"I don't know the details," I say, "but…"

"Forget it, I shouldn't have asked, even if your mother encouraged me to run. He's your cousin."

"He's a bit of an ass."

"Yes. Well." She pauses. "Thank you for being less of an ass."

"You don't have to keep thanking me."

"Sorry."

I don't want her to say sorry, either. I mean, I'm the one who's been nursing a little crush on my cousin's fiancée for two years. I don't deserve it.

When we get to the house, I follow her upstairs with a box of plants. Apparently, she's staying in my old bedroom. The thought of her undressing and getting into *my* bed—yeah, that's going to fuck with my head.

Yvonne remains oblivious to my distress as we bring the second load of stuff upstairs.

"I'm not going to unpack much," she says as she opens a box. "I don't intend to stay here for long, but it's not easy to get an apartment right now, so it might take several weeks."

She hangs up some clothes in my old closet, and all I can think about is that fabric caressing her skin. I'm jealous of some fucking fabric.

"But don't worry," she continues, "I won't take advantage of your parents' generosity."

"I'm not worried," I say. "You're too afraid of being a bother to take advantage."

She doesn't speak for a while, and just when I'm about to exit the room, she says, "I'm making a mission statement."

"A mission statement?" Aren't those for, like, nonprofits and corporations?

"I'm still working on it, but something like: To be kind without compromising myself, and to enjoy my single life."

I'm not sure what to say, but I'm saved by my dad's appearance in the doorway.

"Leo." He smiles. "Didn't expect to see you."

"Just helping Yvonne move her stuff." I try not to sound defensive. It's perfectly reasonable for me to be here, right? It's not like he can read my mind and know how desperately I want to touch the strap of her tank top, which has slid off her shoulder.

"Good thing your mother ordered extra food. She'll be home in a few minutes."

When he leaves, Yvonne turns to me. "Your parents keep trying to feed me."

"You're surprised? Your parents don't try to feed you?"

"My mom does, but she also criticizes my weight, so it's complicated. And like you said, I'm afraid of being a bother." She twists her lips downward, and I want to kiss them and make them do other things.

I need to get out of here, but I know my parents won't allow me to leave before dinner.

Ten minutes later, the four of us are sitting in the kitchen, helping ourselves to Szechuan food from the takeout containers in the center of the table. Dad and Yvonne are doing most of the talking, discussing some TV series that I've never watched. My dad will probably enjoy having her around. Not because my parents are one of those couples who don't know what to say to each other now that their kids are grown up; no, my dad just likes being social and isn't bothered by other people in his space.

Once dinner is finished and we've loaded the dishwasher, I decide it's time to head out. After going to the washroom, I step into the front hall...and run straight into Yvonne. She stumbles backward, and I reach out to catch her before she can fall to the carpet.

I'm very, very close to her, one of my arms around her waist. It would be so easy to pull her against me, but I have self-control.

Then I see what's in her hand, and my blood runs cold.

My mom's wallet.

Is she stealing from my parents?

I've been captivated by this beautiful woman, but really, how well do I know her? I helped her leave a wedding and move out of her apartment. That's it. What she's shown me of herself—it could all be an act.

Before I know what I'm doing, I've backed her against the wall...and God, that's not helping, but I can't seem to step away. Her breasts are pressed against my chest. She's about four inches shorter than me, and it would be so easy to dip my head and...

Why? Why do I keep having these thoughts about her?

"It's not what it looks like," she says.

I want to pin her wrists above her head, then kiss her to silence the excuses tumbling out of her mouth. I feel hot all over, and I don't know if it's more rage or lust.

I'm not an angry man. I might get frustrated, I might be grouchy at times, but angry? No. I don't have a temper.

My parents have been nothing but kind to her, though, and this is how she repays them? Sure, I've had my own issues with my mom and dad over the years, but they don't deserve this.

Her cheeks are pink, and I hate that it's so fucking pretty. I hate that it's giving me all sorts of thoughts I shouldn't have, yet I can't help it, not when the length of my body is touching hers. It feels terribly right and terribly wrong at the same time. I itch to slide my fingers into her hair, which ends just below her shoulders; I itch to be both gentle and rough.

When it comes to Yvonne Siu, I have endless desires, even when she's holding my mom's wallet.

"It's not what it looks like?" I say, a bit of a sneer in my voice. "Explain."

"I tried to give your parents cash because they keep feeding me, but they refused." She holds up a red bill. A fifty. "So I thought I'd sneak this into your mom's wallet instead. I swear that's what happened. Please believe me."

She was trying to sneak money *into* my mom's wallet? That sounds like a load of crap.

But I think of the fights I've seen break out at restaurants over who's going to pay. Then there's the fact that my mother never has fifty-dollar bills. She always has cash on her, but not fifties.

"If you give me your mom's email address," Yvonne says, "I can do an e-Transfer."

I chuckle—my parents do not do things like Interac e-Transfers—and some of the adrenaline in my body dissipates.

Not all of it, though.

I want her to beg me for other things. She's breathing heavily, and I wonder if she's feeling some of the lust that I am. It seems unlikely, however, and I take a step back before she becomes aware of my physical reaction to her.

She puts the bill in the wallet and returns it to my mom's purse "Maybe it wasn't the brightest move, but I didn't know how else to force her to accept money."

I exhale and scrub a hand over my face. "Fine. I believe you."

I'm not touching her anymore, but I'm still standing fairly close. For some reason, my feet refuse to move. God, I wish...

With a muttered curse, I finally take another step back, and not a moment too soon. My parents enter the front hall, and I feel like I've been caught drawing on a freshly painted wall. (Even though I wasn't the one responsible for the purple spider—no, that was Jon.) But it's not as if I actually kissed her; I was just thinking about it.

Although my expression is impassive, Yvonne's is full of guilt. Maybe being so close to me did give her certain thoughts after all?

No, she looks guilty because she was caught digging through my mom's purse.

At least, I'm pretty sure that's the only reason.

Chapter 8

Yvonne

Look, I know that putting money in Lynne's wallet was a bit intrusive. Desperate to show how much I appreciate what she's done for me, I acted like we're more familiar than we actually are. It's not as if she's my own mother.

But when I think back to my silly attempt to show my appreciation, it brings another image to mind: Leo's face, right above mine, demanding to know why I had his mom's wallet in my hand. He was pissed—I'd never seen him pissed before—but there was something weirdly thrilling about it. Excitement thrummed through my veins, especially when he touched me, as if I liked his closeness and wished he'd pull me closer.

Am I attracted to Leo? I was supposed to marry someone else two days ago.

No, my feelings are just mixed up because of everything that happened. That's all. That's the only reason I had such a strong reaction to him; my body and brain are in a general state of confusion these days.

Yet the memory won't leave my mind, and I don't have a great night's sleep.

Tuesday morning, I have a strong cup of coffee before finding the perfect spots for each of my plants in my temporary bedroom. Then I water the ones that need it, using the little watering can that I stashed in a tote bag at my old apartment.

I'll never go back there again.

I'm immediately overcome with a sense of loss. Not because I'm especially attached to the apartment where I lived for the past two years, ever since we got engaged. Not because I miss Carl. But a part of me still misses my old life, misses knowing where I was headed. I don't like feeling unmoored. I had my future all mapped out, and now I have no idea what next week will bring; the uncertainty is terrifying.

I feel like I ought to care more about my ex-fiancé. We were together for a few years. Shouldn't I miss him, at least a little? What's wrong with me?

And why did I feel that brief sizzle of electricity with his cousin?

I don't let myself examine those questions too closely, a little afraid of the answers.

I can't wait to go back to work tomorrow. I badly need a sense of normalcy.

Unfortunately, returning to the office doesn't give me what I want because I have to tell everyone what happened.

My mom tried to convince me to invite my colleagues to my nuptials, but I said no, and unlike with other things, she didn't push too hard. I wouldn't expect to be invited to these people's weddings; I hope they didn't feel upset that they weren't invited to mine. I read more than one article online that suggested I wasn't committing a massive faux pas by doing this.

"How was the wedding?" asks one colleague as I put my food in the fridge.

"Uh, I didn't get married," I mumble.

Suddenly, it feels like everyone is in the break room, and the looks on their faces...I think they assume I got jilted.

"I was the one who called it off," I clarify, without mentioning that I "called it off" at the last possible moment by running back up the aisle.

I hate having my personal and professional lives mix, but my colleagues knew I was taking a few days off for the wedding, and I'm no longer wearing the ring. I couldn't avoid the issue forever.

Ignoring the curious looks, I head to my desk and open up a spreadsheet. I might not know how to handle everything happening in my life right now, but spreadsheets? I can manage those.

At lunch, I consider sending a text to Tracey, but after typing and deleting three different messages, I give up and look at my favorite houseplant accounts instead.

The commute is longer than what I'm used to. A week ago, I lived a seven-minute walk from the subway station, but now, I have to take a bus from Finch, and by the time I get off, I'm nauseous and hungry.

When I step inside Howie and Lynne's house, it smells delicious. I freeze in the front hall, remembering what happened here on Monday with Leo, then shake my head to rid it of that thought. I enter the kitchen to find Howie at the stove, stirring something in a wok. It's nice to return after a day of work to someone else's cooking. I'm not used to it. Howie told me yesterday that they'd always make enough dinner for me, unless I said I was going out, and even though I protested, he insisted.

It would be much less work than feeding multiple teenage boys, I was told, which is what they did for years.

"Do you need any help?" I ask him.

"Ah no, you relax. Almost done."

You see, this is why I felt the need to stuff cash in Lynne's wallet! They won't let me do anything other than my own laundry, even though I dumped their nephew in a humiliating fashion.

Does Gladys know I'm staying here? I doubt it. There's no way she'd approve.

The three of us sit down to eat ten minutes later, and I make sure I compliment the food, which is quite tasty.

After dinner, I stand up and say, "I'm going out. I'll be back in a few hours."

Lynne opens her mouth—to ask where I'm going, I assume—but then closes it. I guess she's decided it's not her business. Even if I did want to tell her, I don't think I'd be able to get the words out.

I'm going to visit my parents.

"Do you need a car?" Howie asks.

I park the Camry in the driveway of my parents' house and walk toward my doom. I'm not usually so melodramatic, but this isn't usual life. Normally, I'd use my key and walk in, but I ring the doorbell, and when nobody answers, I ring it again. Other than a quick text, I haven't communicated with my parents at all since the wedding that wasn't.

At last, the door swings open, and my dad's angry voice fires, "What do you..."

When he sees it's me, he stops talking and walks away.

"It's your daughter," he says as he enters the living room.

This is something he'd do when Tracey didn't behave the way he wanted: he'd talk as though she wasn't his daughter, just Ma's. Like it was all my mother's fault that Tracey hadn't behaved properly.

I'd never heard him speak about *me* that way, though.

Even if this was somewhat anticipated—I knew I'd primarily be speaking with my mother today—it hurts. I spent my life trying to live up to expectations, and in a split second, I blew up that version of myself. Sure, my parents weren't thrilled about me living with Carl before marriage, but since we were engaged, their disapproval was muted.

I slip off my shoes and put on a pair of slippers as I wait for my mom. She walks toward me and surprises me with an embrace, but before I can return it, she pulls back.

"How could you do that to us?" she asks.

"I'm so sorry, Ma. I should have called it off sooner."

"You shouldn't have called it off at all!"

I follow her into the kitchen, where she starts cutting up some fruit.

"I was so ashamed," she says, "and all the money we spent? Aiyah!"

"I'll work on repaying you," I say quickly. "I'll transfer a thousand dollars to your account tonight, as a start."

My mother snorts, then whacks a cantaloupe in a menacing way before scooping out the seeds. "Nothing can make up for how you embarrassed us. He would have been a good son-in-law, and you threw it all away—why?"

"I'd rather be single than be married to him."

She clucks her tongue. "How will you have children now? You're too old to start over."

Thanks, Ma.

"I'm really not that old. Besides…" I clear my throat. "I don't want children."

It's the first time I've said that out loud, and it's a relief to finally put the words out there. Having kids was just one of those things I assumed I'd do. It's not something that everyone does, of course, but it was what my parents imagined for me.

When I pictured having kids with Carl, I knew I'd be doing most of the parenting. But I eventually realized it wasn't simply that I didn't want kids with him; I didn't want kids with anyone.

There's a part of me that worried I wouldn't be a good parent, I'm not going to lie. I didn't have the greatest examples when growing up. Still, I think I could do an okay job of it.

But I'm not interested in that future.

"You don't *want* children," Ma repeats, as though it's ridiculous and she can't believe what I'm saying.

"That's right."

I don't mention that if she's so concerned about grandchildren, her other daughter is pregnant. I'd never reveal that without Tracey's permission.

Ma smacks a plate with cantaloupe and orange slices in front of me.

"Eat," she says.

I'm too scared to disobey her. I bite into a piece of cantaloupe, half expecting I won't be able to taste anything, but it's delicious. "This is a good one."

Ma glowers at me. "I just don't understand why you had to run."

"I had to do it for *me*."

"It's like you don't care about your family."

"I care," I say, "but I couldn't go through with it."

"After all the work we did!"

"Like I said, I should have called it off sooner." But I was scared, and there was the whole sunk cost thing. In addition to the money, I'd invested so much time in that relationship.

When I couldn't sleep last night, I spent half an hour reading about the sunk cost fallacy and how we tend to cling to existing relationships, even if they're not great.

"He cheated on me."

The words tumble out of my mouth, even though I hadn't intended to tell my mother about that. It's so painful, and I've barely spoken about it at all.

I should have ended the engagement then, especially since I was already having a few doubts after what happened with Francine. But despite his lackluster apologies, I didn't. No, instead I wondered why I wasn't enough for him, and if I wasn't enough for Carl, how could I hope to do better?

I don't think he expected to get caught, but he also seemed confident that I wouldn't leave him because of it. I was the sweet little fiancée who'd make him dinner and keep my mouth shut.

How did I find out?

She told me.

She didn't know he was engaged, and when she learned the truth, she found me on social media and informed me that my fiancé was having an affair. She said if I didn't believe her, she could send screenshots of his texts, and for some reason, I felt the need to see proof. But as Carl had correctly surmised, I forgave him and didn't call off the wedding.

Until the very last minute.

I realized I'd had it backward: I was too good for him, not the other way around.

Ma sits down across from me. She's moving slowly, like she has the weight of the world on her shoulders. "Men have different appetites from us."

"I can't believe you're excusing his behavior."

Except I totally can.

I stuff a piece of orange in my mouth, and as the juice trickles down my fingers, I examine my mother. Will I look like her when I'm sixty-one? Will my hair be mostly black, threaded with strands of gray? Will I grow thinner as I age? Will there be pronounced lines on my face between my carefully groomed eyebrows?

Will I be married to a man who cheated on me?

I'm suddenly sure that's why she's saying this, and it doesn't shock me as much as it should. She's trying to convince herself as much as she's trying to convince me; she wants to believe she did the right thing.

I don't say any of that, of course. I've said enough today.

I stand up. "I should get going."

"Where are you staying?"

"With a friend."

"Which one?" she asks.

"I won't give you more reasons to yell at me."

"I'm not yelling!"

Ha.

I'm not used to being the reason my mom's pissed. I want to soothe her, but what could I even say?

I go to the front hall and put on my shoes.

When I return to the house that's my temporary home, Howie and Lynne are watching a drama. Her head is resting on his shoulder, and that shouldn't be in any way odd, but I'm not used to older couples showing affection.

That's what I want, when I'm in my sixties. To be more like them than my own parents.

Except I don't want kids, and right now, marriage is the last thing I wish to think about, but one day, it could be nice to have someone.

Eventually, Lynne notices me in the doorway to the living room. She pauses the show.

"Are you okay, Yvonne?" she asks.

"I went to see my parents. My dad wouldn't talk to me." There's a jolt of pain in my chest at the words, which annoys me. I shouldn't expect my father to be different, yet I never completely stopped hoping. "My mother..."

It's not like I truly expected her to act differently, either, but it would have been nice if she was at least pleased to see that I'm okay.

But in truth, it's like I'm in free fall. I'm relieved, I'm happy, I'm distressed, all at once.

It averages out to "okay," though.

This is why averages don't tell the whole story. Like, if you have five people, and four of them make $5,000 a year and one made $5,000,000 a year, the average salary in that small group would be over a million dollars. Knowing just the average and nothing else doesn't give you a real grasp of the situation.

So "okay" is far from the whole story, but in some ways, it's true. I'm not entirely comfortable with my decision, but I think I made the right one.

"She's still angry with me," I say at last.

I'm braced for platitudes. *They'll come around soon. I'm sure they're just worried about you and don't know how to express it.*

But Lynne doesn't say those things, and it's refreshing. She knows that sometimes, people simply don't come around, and wishing for it doesn't make it true.

"You can watch with us." She gestures to the other end of the couch.

"We're on the fourth episode," Howie points out.

"Yes, you can explain the plot to her while I make tea."

"No, no, you shouldn't," I say. "It's been a long day. A long week." I force a chuckle. "I'm going upstairs to get ready for bed."

Lynne nods. "By the way, I did notice the money. You didn't need to, but thank you."

As I trudge up the stairs, I think, *Why can't they be my parents?*

Except if they actually were my parents, I may well feel otherwise. Once again, I find myself thinking of Leo, wondering what his relationship with his mom and dad is like, before recalling the press of his body against mine. My breath quickens at the memory. His lips were so close, and I'm not used to feeling tempted like that, to wishing for things I have no business wishing for.

I just hope my feelings level out soon.

Chapter 9

Leo

AFTER DOING MY STANDARD exercises for leg day, I get on the treadmill, but forty minutes later, it still doesn't feel like enough. A week of work is behind me, and I might be physically exhausted from my workout, but no matter how much I sweat, I can't wipe Yvonne from my mind.

Why should you? a little voice asks. *She's single now.*

Yeah, and I'm sure she's in no place to change that. I know she simply sees me as a friend, while I see her as the woman I'd happily sketch for weeks on end because she's so stunning. The fact that she was willing to ditch the safe life she had planned—well, that makes her even more alluring.

After sixty minutes, I decide to stop hoping for the impossible. Time to accept that she'll be on my mind no matter what. I drive home and hop in the shower, where I picture the water running over her skin instead.

By the time I've eaten leftovers for dinner, it's eight o'clock. I take out my tablet, determined to work on this cover for an hour before I watch something.

I don't have the most exciting life. I used to go out more when I was younger, but now, I'm content to spend Friday night alone in my apartment. It did get to me at the beginning of the pandemic, though. Not the fact that I couldn't see anyone in person—sometimes that's preferable, to be honest—but the fact that I was spending so much time in my four-hundred-square-foot apartment.

I've been working at my small desk, which is crammed in the corner opposite my bed, for a grand total of five minutes when my phone vibrates. Normally, I'd ignore it, but what if it's Yvonne? The thought shouldn't make my pulse speed up, but it does.

I check. It's just a stupid message from Jon, and that annoys me more than it should.

I return to my work without replying, but three seconds later, my phone buzzes again.

"For fuck's sake," I mutter, but I look at my phone, just in case.

YVONNE: Hey! What are your plans for the weekend?

I stare at the words, half-convinced I'm imagining this, before turning to Francine. "You know her better than I do. Why is she asking?"

Then I realize I'm talking to a goddamn plant. I asked Francine a question even though she can't reply.

But plants like when you speak to them, right? I swear I've read that before. Does Yvonne talk to Francine? Probably. Perhaps Francine misses it, and if I want her to thrive, I should speak to her even more.

Or do plants only like it if you speak to them in a certain way, and asking questions about your cousin's ex-fiancée doesn't count?

I think I'm losing it. I need a drink.

I pour myself a rum and Coke, which I sip as I try to figure out what to say to Yvonne. After five minutes of staring at my phone, I settle on the perfect response.

ME: Not too much

"What do you think?" I ask Francine.

She doesn't speak or give any indication that she's heard my question...again, because she's a goddamn plant.

YVONNE: Would you like to hang out on Saturday? I want to stay out for much of the day so I don't bother your parents. It's so nice of them to let me stay here.

ME: Sure. What are you thinking?

YVONNE: Let's go out for brunch

The restaurant that Yvonne has selected is a little different from any brunch I've had in the past. It's a Middle Eastern restaurant with a patio out front, where people are sipping a variety of caffeinated drinks in dainty serving vessels.

I'm certainly not *dainty*.

Yvonne isn't here yet. Since I think she'll appreciate sitting outside—she mentioned the patio in one of her texts—I ask the hostess for the last outdoor table. Only one of the chairs is under the shade of the umbrella, so I take the other one as I open my menu and wait for my not-date.

But having brunch on a patio like this? It feels like it should be a date.

When Yvonne walks up to the restaurant, she looks around the patio for a moment, and a smile graces her face when she sees me. She waves before walking over.

"Hi!" She leans in and gives me a hug.

I don't think of the time I backed her against the wall at my parents' house and nearly kissed her... No, I don't think about that at all. Haven't thought about it since.

Yeah, right.

Yvonne takes a seat. She looks more relaxed than she did last Saturday.

"I didn't bring Francine," I say. "I wasn't sure she'd like being in a hot car while we ate."

"She's doing okay, though?"

"Yes."

"You're following her schedule?"

"Yes."

"You're talking to her?"

"What? No." It's far too embarrassing to admit I've spoken to something that can't understand me. I'm also flustered because Yvonne's words make me feel like she's been watching me, and I'd hate for her to know how much I think about her.

"That's okay," she says. "It might be a little change from what Francine is used to, but I'm sure she'll adapt, though she does like her lullabies every night."

For a split second, I consider asking which lullabies so I can keep up her routine, but I shut that shit down fast. Surely, it's not normal to consider singing to a plant owned by your cousin's ex-fiancée.

Yeah, I just have to keep reminding myself of who Yvonne is.

I did text Carl a few days ago to see how he's doing. I felt like I owed him that much. He didn't respond.

"I'm kidding!" She laughs. "You should see your scowl."

"Thanks."

"About the lullabies, I mean. I do talk to Francine."

Of course she does. And, of course, I find that cute.

The server comes around with my Turkish coffee, and Yvonne asks for a latte. We lapse into silence as we study our menus. I know what I'm getting, but I keep staring at the menu so I don't stare at my dining companion. She ends up ordering the pancakes, which come with sour cherry sauce and other things.

"So," she says, once she has her latte in hand. "What do you usually do on the weekend?"

I shrug. "Work out. Waste time."

"I need ideas for my exciting single life." She frowns. "Wait. Are you single? I just assumed, since I've never seen you with anyone else, but if you're not ready to tell your family yet, I understand. I won't say anything to your parents, don't worry."

"I'm single."

"You make it sound so thrilling."

"It is. Very thrilling," I say, my voice deliberately dry.

She laughs again, her lips tipping up in a way that's unfairly appealing. Just the sight and sound of her laughter is enough to make me smile, and that won't do. I try to hide my face behind my dainty coffee cup, but when I take a gulp, I get some coffee grounds and start hacking. Goddammit.

Yvonne hands over my water glass, and when my fingers accidentally brush against hers, that doesn't help matters. I'm a mess around this woman.

"I also...do some work," I say, to take my mind off the feel of her hand. "I have a side business. Illustrations for fantasy book covers."

Maybe it sounds very specific, but it's not a full-time job. Since it doesn't need to pay all my bills, I can focus on the sort of things I like. I started doing it when I was bored in 2020. Got Evan to give me advice on how to do the financial stuff properly so the CRA doesn't come after me...hopefully.

"Oh!" she says. "That's cool. Can you show me some of your work?"

I take out my phone and pull up the portfolio page on my website.

"Wow. These are really impressive, Leo. Do you draw them on a tablet?"

I nod, feeling a bit uncomfortable with her praise.

She scrolls through the page for a minute before the server returns with our food. Yvonne hands my phone back and digs into her thick pancakes, which are dusted with powdered sugar. Brunch is often an excuse for people to consume dessert for a meal, and I can't say I understand.

My platter, on the other hand, contains a variety of cheeses, meats, boiled eggs, sliced vegetables, dried fruits, and spreads, to be eaten with flatbread and something similar to a bagel with a very large hole.

"That looks so good." Yvonne has been easily delighted today, but then she says, "Sorry for asking you to hang out with me."

"You don't need to apologize." I might be drinking coffee out of a dainty cup and sitting on a dainty patio chair, but she has no reason to be sorry.

"It's just...I don't know who I can talk to. Take my bridesmaids, for example. Two of them don't approve of what I did at *all*. Another is my cousin, who's always busy on the weekends with her family, and Shauna…"

"What did she do?"

"She's been supportive, but I feel like I've neglected our friendship over the years. Haven't made time for her like I should have, and it feels wrong to ask for her for much now."

"What do you want her to do?"

"Just hang out with me."

I don't generally have much advice for such issues, but… "Then tell her that. It doesn't need to be more complicated."

She sighs. "I'm embarrassed by the past, but yeah, I should get over it. By the way, do you have my veil?"

"It's in my car. I'll get it for you when we're finished."

"Shauna said I should be a zombie bride for Halloween. The veil could come in handy."

I kinda like this friend. "Text her. I can drive you to see her after this."

"You don't know where she lives."

"True," I say. "If she lives in Oakville, I might take that back."

"It's about a fifteen-minute drive from here. Dependent on traffic, of course."

I gesture for her to go ahead and text. I mean, what the fuck else am I going to do today? It seems a little dangerous to spend more time with her, but it's just a short drive. It's not like anything's going to happen.

She flashes me a brilliant smile that I don't deserve, then digs her phone out of her purse.

"Try my pancakes," she says as she's typing. "They're really good."

"No."

"It's almost like dessert."

"I don't like dessert."

Her head jerks up. "You don't like dessert? We had ice cream together."

"I didn't care that it was sweet. Just wanted something cold."

"You know, I've heard that such people exist—people who don't crave sweets—but I've never met one in the wild before."

In the wild, indeed.

My lips twitch, and I hold up my hands. "Well, here I am."

"I'll have to do some tests."

"What sort of tests?"

Oh God. Is there a hint of flirtation in my voice?

"Will you feed me sugar cubes," I say, "and see what happens?"

She smiles and sets down her phone. When it buzzes a second later, she picks it up again. "Shauna's free. You sure you don't mind taking me?"

I finish my coffee. "I'm sure."

"Thank you," she says, "and thank you for meeting me here. I've wanted to try this place for a while, but my weekends were filled with wedding planning, and Carl wasn't interested in going."

"No problem," I grunt, but I need to start spending less time with her. It's putting impossible thoughts in my head.

It's easy to hang out with Yvonne. She keeps the conversation going, and the way she smiles and says she's never met anyone in the wild like me...

Yeah, I really should pull back.

Chapter 10

Yvonne

I HAVEN'T BEEN HERE in a decade, and there have been some changes in that time. The garage door is green instead of red. The driveway is no longer full of cracks. The tree in the front yard is gone—I remember Shauna mentioning that it had been damaged in a windstorm.

Whenever I've seen her in the past several years, it's never been at her house, even though I spent quite a bit of time here in high school. Her house was more comfortable than my own: there wasn't as much yelling, and the silences weren't quite so loaded.

Shauna and I went to different elementary schools, and we met in grade nine. Her house is an eight-minute bike ride from where my parents still live. I know exactly how long it takes because I used to do it regularly, though I haven't ridden a bike in years now.

She comes out to meet me—she must have heard the car pull up—and I wave to Leo before he backs out of the driveway.

"Who's that?" she asks.

"Leo," I say. "Carl's cousin. He's the wedding guest who helped me escape after I collided with his car. I'm staying with his parents until I find an apartment."

"You're staying with your ex's aunt and uncle?"

"Yeah."

"Are you sure you don't want to stay here?" Shauna asks as we walk inside and slip off our shoes. "I don't think my mom and dad would mind. They like you."

I think of all the time I used to spend with Shauna, and I'm filled with regret that I didn't prioritize our relationship in recent years.

"I'm sorry," I say as I step onto the gray carpet, the one I remember from back in the day. I wouldn't have recalled the color of the carpet off the top of my head, but when I see that it's gray, it looks right.

She frowns. "What are you sorry for?"

It's awkward to talk about this directly, but I can't just push the past aside.

"For neglecting our friendship," I say unsteadily. "When I asked you to be in my wedding party, I hadn't seen you in two years."

Shauna folds her arms over her chest. "Well, there's this thing called COVID-19."

"But it's not like we were having Zoom chats or texting much. You seemed surprised that I wanted you to be a bridesmaid."

"Yes, well. It felt like you were building this perfect little life, and I didn't belong in it."

There's bitterness in her voice, as there should be. It hurts, but at the same time, I'm relieved that she feels she can be honest.

"You're right," I say. "I was an idiot."

"You still haven't told me what happened with Carl."

I follow her into the kitchen, which is exactly as I remember. She starts making coffee. I had a latte not long ago, but I'm not going to complain.

"Did you like him?" I find myself asking as we sit down at the table.

"He seemed fine, but I had no idea what he was like when it was just the two of you."

"Well, I had to do most of the chores. I had to..." I glance around.

"Don't worry, my parents won't hear. They're away for the weekend."

"Your parents are away for the weekend?"

She laughs. "I know. They go on monthly dates and the occasional weekend getaway."

My parents would never, and it's hard to imagine her parents doing that, too. Leo's parents, on the other hand, seem more likely to do such a thing—I can see Howie suggesting it.

"I guess it's easier now." Her gaze slides to the left, toward the downstairs bedroom. "Now that Bà isn't here, I mean, though it's weird to think of it that way."

I reach across the table and squeeze her hand.

She clears her throat. "So. Back to Carl."

"Right. He...I also had to get myself off, most of the time." I cover my mouth. I can't believe I just said that.

Shauna's eyes widen. I don't know if it's more because I never discuss these things—she was always more comfortable than I was—or if it's the fact that he wasn't attentive in bed.

"When I thought of our future together," I say, not wishing to dwell on that, "I just felt dread. He wanted me to change my name." Traditionally, Chinese women don't change their names upon marriage, even if my mom did when she came to Canada. But Carl said it would be better this way, better for me to have the same name as our children, and I felt like I had to acquiesce. "He wanted kids. He wanted me to be a stay-at-home mom until they started school. That all fit into the life I thought

I desired, but I started doubting it, and I realized I don't really want to be a parent."

"No?" Shauna sounds a little surprised but not judgmental. She gets up and pours us coffee. She adds soy milk to her own and slides the black stuff toward me.

"Thanks." I take a bracing sip of coffee.

We're silent for a moment, and I think of all that has changed and all that hasn't.

"You should get laid," she declares. "Sleep with someone who actually wants to give you an orgasm."

An image of Leo pops into my brain, but I quickly push it aside.

"It *does* take me a long time," I say.

She rolls her eyes. "Please. You still deserve to get off like…sixty-nine percent of the time. Maybe you have the occasional quickie that doesn't quite get you all the way there, but it sounds like Carl didn't put in much effort—and not just in the bedroom. So, fuck him."

I open my mouth, ready to tell Shauna that Carl also cheated on me, but I can't do it, not in this house that's familiar in a distant sort of way. Though she's on my side, would she think I was too pathetic for not dropping him immediately?

"So, how have you been?" I ask instead.

She wags her finger at me. "No, we're still talking about you."

"But—"

"You left someone at the altar last weekend. I think you still deserve all the attention." She tilts her head. "What about Leo? Maybe you should sleep with him. He's kinda hot."

Oh God. How embarrassing. It's like she knows how often he appears in my thoughts, even though I wish he wouldn't.

"How would you know?" I ask, making an effort to sound calm. To not sound like someone who was a little turned on when he backed me against a wall. "You saw him through a car window. And he's Carl's cousin—"

"Carl doesn't have to know. I assume you're not looking for a relationship?"

"Definitely not."

"So?"

She makes it sound easy, but I've never slept with someone I'm not dating. I don't know how I'd bring it up. Besides...

"He's not my type," I say, though it feels like a lie now.

"Are you sure? Your face looks a little flushed."

"Because I'm not used to talking about sex!"

Shauna smirks, and I realize with a jolt that it's been a while since she's teased me...and I missed it.

"Tell me what your type is, then," she says. "Maybe I know someone."

"My type has hair."

Leo shaves his head. It's not something I've ever been particularly attracted to before.

Or now. I'm not attracted to him now, either.

Okay, perhaps I should stop lying to myself. When I think of him sitting across from me on the patio and scowling at the sun—he'd graciously given me the chair that was shaded—there's an odd stirring in my belly. He's rather handsome. In the past, I've been drawn to men who were more polished, but there's something compelling about him.

Will you feed me sugar cubes and see what happens? He'd asked it with a ghost of a smile. I don't think he'd meant for me to think of his lips on my fingers, but I did. It flustered me, though I think I hid it well.

And now, I'm picturing his head between my thighs. I can't seem to help it.

"Whatever my feelings," I say, pushing those images aside, "I'm sure he doesn't think of me like that."

"He stayed with you after you ran."

"Because he's nice and friendly. And probably felt bad about my collision with his car, even if it was my fault."

Except Leo doesn't have a particularly "friendly" vibe.

"Why was he driving you around today?" Shauna asks.

"I asked him to go out for brunch."

"Interesting that you asked him...and he agreed."

"Like I told you," I say feebly, "he's friendly."

"Mm." She raises her eyebrows.

Okay, we need to stop talking about Leo Mok.

"For the rest of today, I'm all yours," I tell Shauna. "And I promise, I won't grow distant on you again. I know you might not believe me right now, and that's okay."

"You've gotta make it up to me."

"How can I do that?"

"You have to do whatever I say for Halloween. Bring me your dress and let me make your costume, and then we're going to whatever party I decide."

Usually, I think months and years in advance, but in the past week, I've had to take everything one day at a time. Halloween seems impossibly far away, even if it's only two months. Still, I'm happy to plan this much.

I pull the veil out of my purse. "I'll bring you the dress next time."

"Why were you carrying around your wedding veil?"

"I left it in Leo's car, and he returned it to me today." So much for not talking about Leo. "He's still taking care of my snake plant, though, because he was afraid she wouldn't like the hot car."

"Yeah, I'm sure this boy is just being friendly."

The fact that she calls him a "boy" makes me giggle.

"So, what do you want to do now?" Shauna asks.

I used to struggle when she asked this question. When it came to the big things, I was always thinking of what others wanted for me, but even for smaller things, it could be hard. I wanted to please other people.

I try to set that aside. This is a new phase in my life.

"Let's go to the mall."

Yes, it's a new phase in my life, and I'm celebrating that by doing something I would have done back when I was a young teenager.

It's been a little while since I last went to a mall—any mall—and probably a decade since I went to this one. Though a few of the stores I remember are here, a lot of them have changed, and the mall looks like it's seen better days. I still manage to find a nice shirt, one that I never would have bought in high school—like many teens, I was uncomfortable with my body, and besides, my parents wouldn't have approved—but I also wouldn't have bought it even just a few months ago. It's bright and clingy. Too clingy to hide the fact that my stomach isn't flat, but who cares? I shouldn't think of that as a flaw.

After the mall, we pick up a pizza and take it back to Shauna's, where we watch movies and drink wine. I'm definitely not on my pre-wedding diet anymore.

"You want to stay over?" she asks.

For a split second, I feel like I have to ask my parents for permission...but I'm twenty-nine, and my dad's not even speaking to me. I don't need permission, though I do text Lynne so she doesn't worry about me.

"You can stay in Bà's old room," Shuana says. "No need to sleep on my floor."

We're halfway through *Ever After* and most of the way through the wine when my phone buzzes three times. I pick it up and see a photo of my sister holding a small bundle in her arms.

"Oh my God!" I shriek. "Tracey had her baby."

"*What?*" Shauna pauses the movie. "Hold on. Your sister was pregnant?"

"Yeah. I only found out last week. Our parents don't know, so don't tell anyone."

She mimes zipping her mouth, and we look at the picture of my sister and my nephew. I can't believe I have a nephew! He's wrinkly and funny-looking—I've never been particularly enamored with newborns—but a wave of fondness washes over me.

And then I read the words.

They're already home from the hospital. He was born *two days* ago.

My happiness is tempered by irritation that she didn't tell me sooner—this is my sister!—but I shouldn't be annoyed. Even if she was good to me on what was supposed to be my wedding day, we're not close, and I can't help the ache in my chest. I long to have more of a sisterly bond with her, and while I can't change our past, I can do better going forward. I won't be pushy; I'll respect her choices.

ME: Congrats!! Does he have a name yet?

TRACEY: Still figuring it out

ME: Let me know if you need anything.

ME: I can bring you food or pick up something from the store.

ME: Or do laundry.

I don't expect her to take me up on any of that, and I don't ask to see him as soon as possible. I want her to have time to get settled at home.

But I do look forward to meeting him.

It's almost midnight, and I'm in Shauna's grandmother's old room. As a teenager, I saw more of her than I did of Shauna's mom and dad, who were often working. But her grandma would cook for us and ask me questions in broken English. When she passed away in 2020, I attended the online funeral.

I desperately want to sleep, but my mind refuses to be quiet. It's constantly jumping from one thing to another. From the time we tried to teach Bà to use Google, to the time I asked Tracey why she left her school projects to the night before. (She told me to fuck off and got in trouble.) I picture Lindsay Lohan dressed as a zombie bride in *Mean Girls*—the first movie we watched tonight—and I wonder what I'll look like at Halloween.

Between Lynne, Howie, Leo, and Shauna, I've had little time to myself today, and I don't like being alone with my thoughts now. I pick up my phone and text Leo. *You up?*

When he replies, not ten seconds later, I smile.

LEO: yes

ME: I can't sleep

LEO: My old bedroom not treating you well?

ME: I didn't know it used to be your room, but I'm not there tonight. Still at Shauna's. Thanks again for the ride.

LEO: you're welcome

ME: What are you up to?

There's no response for a while, and just when I'm about to set my phone aside, I receive a photo of a tablet. On the tablet is a drawing of Francine.

I shouldn't read too much into it. Artists draw all sorts of things. Still lifes of fruit, for example. Earlier today, I came across a nice painting of a Tim Hortons cup and donut online.

Yet for some reason, I'm tickled that Leo drew a picture of my plant, that he spent more than three seconds looking at her.

ME: OMG. That's beautiful. Do you often draw houseplants?

LEO: No. I don't have any of my own. I'll bring Francine back on Tuesday.

ME: No rush. You don't have to make a trip just for that.

LEO: I'm not. My mom invited us over for
dinner.

I assume "us" means him and his brothers, and I'm more
excited than I should be at the idea of seeing Leo again. My face
flames as I think of my conversation with Shauna.

I shove those thoughts out of my mind as I look at the picture
of my new nephew. I don't need to be having inappropriate
thoughts about Carl's cousin when there are more important
things to care about.

Yvonne's Search History

- Lindsay Lohan filmography

- variegated monstera

- watermelon peperomia

- pottery classes Toronto

- apartments Toronto

- average price apartment Toronto

- tips for finding affordable apartment

- why are search results so bad these days

- why am I attracted to my ex's cousin

Chapter 11

Leo

MY PLANS TO PULL back from Yvonne were blown apart when I got home from brunch on Saturday and realized I'd missed a call from my mother, inviting me for dinner in a few days. I didn't have a good excuse to decline, so I said I'd come.

Besides, I have to return Francine at some point.

I walk up the path to the house and open the door. I'm momentarily taken aback when I step inside and Yvonne is right there.

"Hi!" she says.

We stare at each other for an awkward moment.

Goddammit. I swear there's more, for lack of a better word, *sparkle* each time I see her. Not getting married looks good on her. Her hair is partially pulled back, and she's wearing jeans and a T-shirt. Nothing fancy, but that doesn't mean I don't want to plant a kiss on those pink lips.

Goddammit.

"Evan, Max, and Kim are already here," she says. "I'm just helping your dad in the kitchen. You can take Francine upstairs to my room—I mean, your old room."

I nod before slipping off my shoes and ascending the stairs. I set Francine on the small desk in the bedroom, and next to her, I place a small wrapped gift.

"What's that?" Max is standing in the doorway.

I suddenly feel ridiculous. I just wrapped it because I thought Yvonne would enjoy unwrapping a gift. Since all the wrapping paper in my closet had either snowmen or reindeer, I needed to buy something new. I shouldn't have been so pleased when I found paper with potted plants on it at Shoppers—I might have even smiled—but I was.

"A picture frame." Not a lie. Underneath that wrapping paper is a frame...with the drawing I did of Francine. I printed it out yesterday. "Yvonne said she needed one."

"Hmm." Max crosses his arms over his chest.

My eldest brother is five years older than me and five inches taller. I can't say we're super close, but we get along fine. He's usually serious and composed, but I can't help thinking of what happened at our cousin Mirabel's wedding in July. Max encountered Kim, with whom he'd had a not-so-spectacular one-night stand, and got wasted. I'd never seen him drunk like that before, and I stupidly thought it would be the right time to fess up about my silly crush. I felt the need to tell someone, and I figured there was no way he'd remember.

He didn't forget, though. He mentioned it the next morning when he was hungover.

But everything seems to have worked out with Kim, based on the fact that she's here tonight.

"What's happening between you and Yvonne?" he asks.

"Nothing," I reply.

"Are you glad she didn't get married?"

"She seems happy...so, yes."

He raises an eyebrow. "She just got out of a serious relationship."

"I'm aware," I say dryly.

"She's in a vulnerable place. Don't take advantage—"

"What the hell?" I explode. Then I drop my voice. "She asked me to take care of her plant, so I did. She asked me to help move her stuff, so I did. She wanted to have brunch—"

"You had brunch together?"

"It was her idea, like I said. I've never touched her." Aside from backing her up against the wall...

Max raises an eyebrow again.

"I never should have told you," I mutter, "but don't worry, I understand nothing can happen. I don't need two engineering degrees to know that."

His face softens—as much as Max's face can soften. "I wouldn't say nothing can *ever* happen, but it certainly can't happen now, when she's trying to get her life in order," he says before heading downstairs.

I'm surprised he doesn't consider a cousin's ex permanently off-limits, and his words give me a foolish glimmer of hope.

I promptly squash it.

"Don't tell Yvonne about that conversation, okay?" I murmur to Francine.

"I hear you're looking for an apartment." Evan reaches for the noodles.

"I am," Yvonne says. "Unfortunately, I don't think I'll find anything for September; the market is terrible. But hopefully, I'll get a place for October." She raises her chopsticks to her lips, and even that simple motion looks graceful when she does it.

"I'll ask around, see if anyone has any leads."

"That would be great. Thank you."

I glare at my food, feeling a weird sort of jealousy. It's not like helping Yvonne is *my* job.

After we finish eating and clearing the table, Kim brings out the small cake that she brought for dessert. She's about to start cutting it when the doorbell rings.

"It's probably the kid behind us," Dad says. "He sometimes kicks the ball over the fence and into our yard. Can you get it, Leo?"

I head to the front door. Before I can get there, the doorbell rings again. I guess the kid really is impatient to get his ball back, but he hasn't even given us a chance to answer.

I'm a little irritated as I swing open the door, but I try not to look it, reminding myself that it's just a kid and I might have done the same thing at his age.

But the person standing on the doorstep isn't a child.

It's my aunt.

"Is she here?" Auntie Gladys demands.

"Who?" I ask, but I know the answer.

Before I can stop her, she marches inside without bothering to remove her shoes.

Chapter 12

Yvonne

"Ha!" Carl's mom points a finger at me. "She *is* here. My sources were right."

Sources. Like she's some kind of reporter.

"How could you do this to me?" Gladys turns to Lynne.

"Why are you blaming her?" Howie says genially, stepping between the two of them. "It's my house, too."

"How could you let her do this?"

"It's not like we're harboring a fugitive. Yvonne just decided she didn't want to get married."

I hate being the cause of drama. When I was a kid, it was Tracey who caused drama while I watched from the sidelines, occasionally feeling a bit smug. But if I'd learned to stick up for myself when I was younger, I wouldn't be in this mess now.

I step toward the woman who almost became my mother-in-law. "I apologize. This is my fault, and I will take responsibility for it. I should have called it off earlier, rather than rushing from the altar."

"You call that an apology?" she says.

I press on. "Lynne and Howie have been very kind to let me stay here while I look for an apartment. I didn't have many options. Please don't be mad at them."

Gladys sniffs. "You know how embarrassing it was? I'll have to find a new church!"

"I'm sorry." I look down. "I really do feel badly for the fallout, but I just couldn't go through with it."

When I dare to look up, she's glaring daggers at me, and for a split second, I wonder if I made a mistake.

I picture being back in that apartment with Carl. Picking up after him. Shoving down my frustration when he made decisions without asking for my input...except for the wedding. That was all on *me*.

The thought makes me cringe.

If only I'd called off the wedding when I found out he was cheating, then at least we would have gotten some of the money back. Gladys might still have felt embarrassed, but not like this. Howie and Lynne wouldn't have been dragged into it.

Maybe I should tell Gladys that her precious son cheated on me, but it's against my instincts to air that sort of dirty laundry. I also fear that, like my own mother, she simply wouldn't care. *It's just the way men are.* Gladys always makes excuses for Carl, and I expect she'd continue to do so.

I glance at Leo. His hand is clenched at his side. I will my cheeks not to turn pink as all my inappropriate thoughts about him return.

"Would you like some cake?" Howie asks his sister-in-law. He speaks pleasantly, pretending to be oblivious to the tension in the room. "Kim brought it. It looks very good."

"I'm the reason that Max has a girlfriend." Gladys points to herself. "This is—"

"Okay, that's enough." Howie leads her out of the dining room.

"Fine! Don't expect me to ever come back!"

"I'm sorry," I say to Lynne later. Everyone else has left, and I'm helping her tidy up.

She waves this off. "Stop saying you're sorry all the time. It's fine."

"I know you and Gladys never got along, but—"

"She said she's never coming back. This is the best thing to happen to me in ages." Lynne's lips twitch.

I stare at her and try not to think about how her expression reminds me of Leo.

"Ah, don't look at me like that," she says. "Gladys will get desperate to talk to someone, and she'll call me in a month or two like nothing happened. But I'll enjoy the peace until then."

"Your nice family dinner—"

"Yvonne." She speaks my name firmly, like she means business. "You can stop."

Now I feel the need to apologize for the fact that I keep apologizing, but I snap my mouth shut and give her a brisk nod.

When I open the door to my temporary room, I can't hold back a smile.

Francine!

In the commotion of earlier, I totally forgot about her.

"It's so nice to see you again," I whisper. "Did Leo take good care of you?"

She looks healthy to me, just as she did when she bloomed. Though some people say flowering snake plants aren't a good sign, I also read that they can flower in the spring under ideal conditions. After hours of research, that was my conclusion about what happened at the end of April. I wonder if she'll bloom again next year.

Then I notice something else that wasn't here before: a small rectangular package, wrapped in cheerful paper with potted succulents. There's no tag on the present, but clearly, it's for me. I have no doubt it's from Leo.

I can't remember the last time I got an unexpected gift. I run my finger over the paper, which he must have picked just for me. There's an odd flutter in my chest as I carefully peel off the tape, and when I set the paper aside, his lovely picture of Francine makes me smile even wider.

Looking at Leo, you wouldn't expect that his art would be *whimsical*, but this is, and it captures her spirit just perfectly. I imagine him sliding the picture into the frame, and for some reason, thinking about the movement of his fingers makes me a little warm. I can't seem to make that warmth go away. Carl's presents were always generic, but this certainly isn't.

I pick up my phone and send a text. *Thank you for the picture!* I nearly add that it wasn't necessary, but I hold myself back as I get comfortable on the bed.

LEO: You're welcome

ME: It's so beautiful. Francine is impressed.

LEO: She should be

I bark out a laugh, delighted. I have no idea what his apartment looks like, but I imagine him sitting on his couch, his lips twitching the tiniest bit.

ME: Her friends are jealous.

LEO: Who are her friends?

ME: Helen, Chloe, and Charlotte are her besties. She's currently feuding with Leora.

This, of course, is a lie; Leora and Francine get along just fine. They used to sit next to each other, back in my old apartment with Carl. He didn't know any of my plants' names, other than Francine's. Since I knew it would annoy him, I never told him.

I don't have to censor myself around Leo in the same way. Then again, we're not in a relationship, and if he gets annoyed with me, it's no big deal.

Actually, that's not true. The idea of him being truly annoyed with me is upsetting. It causes another strange feeling in my chest—why have I been having a bunch of those today? Why am I wishing he'd push me up against a wall again? Or make a comment about sugar cubes?

Weird. Maybe I'm off-balance after Gladys's visit.

I take a couple pictures of my plants and send them to Leo.

LEO: What is the jade plant's name?

ME: Helen

LEO: My parents have one downstairs.

Yes, I noticed that. Jade plants—also known as lucky plants or money trees—are fairly popular houseplants. I'm strangely pleased that he's able to identify any of my plants.

LEO: You didn't want to name her Jade?

ME: No! It's not original at all.

LEO: That's what I would do. Are you saying I'm unoriginal?

ME: Are you saying you'd name your plants if you had any?

LEO: …

ME: Do you want one? I can give you a cutting from Francine. I've never done it before, but I'm curious to try.

LEO: if you like

ME: It'll be a little while before I have a potted plant to give you.

LEO: That's ok. I'm patient.

I wonder if he's patient in other situations. Like, random example, in bed. Would he be patient enough to wait for me to orgasm? Patient enough to help me get there? I think of his hand, clenched at his side, as Gladys was yelling. I imagine those fingers caressing me instead…

Flustered, I tell Leo that I better get going, then check my email. When I discover that one of the apartments I want to look at is no longer available, I silently howl in frustration.

Hmm. Maybe I should work out some of my frustration in another way.

Even though my ex-fiancé rarely got me off, I only took care of myself a couple of times a month. I haven't done it since before the wedding that didn't happen.

Yeah, this must be why I was thinking of Leo's hands on me. It's been a while.

I take out my only sex toy: a small vibrator. I bought this one specifically because it's supposed to be quiet yet powerful, and it didn't disappoint. I'd hoped Carl would be willing to use it on me, but when I brought it up, he took it as an insult.

I get into bed and turn on the toy, and what pops into my mind is...Leo. At first, I imagine him using the vibrator on me as he kisses his way down my body. From my mouth, to my neck, to my collarbone, to my breasts. I know what it's like to feel his body pressed against mine, and that makes this even better.

Then I imagine him slipping his hand between my legs and licking me. Since this is my imagination, he can be very, *very* patient.

And also, very naked.

He looks up at me, his eyes serious yet blazing with heat, but he doesn't neglect my pussy as he holds my gaze; no, his fingers slide inside me, touching me just where I need it.

When he puts his mouth back on me, I buck against his face. To my surprise, I'm really close. Frustratingly close, but I can't seem to get to the peak and...

There.

Pleasure floods my body, and I cover my mouth with my hand as I shudder.

Afterward, I feel a bit weird about it. I just got myself off while fantasizing about my ex-fiancé's cousin. In his old bedroom. What would Leo think?

Heat floods my cheeks once more, and I wonder if he'd like it. He's been perfectly appropriate with me—I mean, aside from the time he backed me against the wall, but he thought I was stealing from his parents—yet now, a collage of his facial expressions forms in my brain. Expressions that suggest he might be a little attracted to me. I was oblivious to it before, but my mind's been everywhere lately. Now it seems clear, though.

Is that the reason he's spent so much time with me?

Maybe Shauna is right: I should sleep with Leo. Of course, nobody could know, but I suspect he'd be good at keeping secrets. He's not the sort to run his mouth.

His mouth.

The next evening, I send him a text.

ME: Want to hang out this weekend?

Chapter 13

Leo

I KEEP TELLING MYSELF that I have to stop seeing Yvonne, but then she says she'll give me a fucking plant and asks me to hang out…

I'm a weak man. I can't refuse her.

She was so thrilled with my drawing that it makes me want to do whatever I can for her. I feel like I live to make her happy.

So now, here we are. Together in my car once again. It's been two weeks since she was supposed to get married…and more than two years since I first met her.

"Why are we going to IKEA?" I ask.

"First of all, because I'm craving Swedish meatballs and now that I don't have to fit into a wedding dress, I'm no longer on a diet."

I refrain from saying she looks perfect as she is.

"I think I've gained three pounds in the last two weeks," she says, "but that's fine. Might have to make some adjustments to the zombie bride costume, but at least it's okay to rip that."

I try not to think of ripping fabric off her body.

"Do you need to buy anything other than meatballs?" I ask.

"A plant stand, and a new pot for Charlotte. I don't want to spend a lot of money because I'll need first and last month's rent for an apartment, plus furniture. I also need to keep paying my parents back for the wedding. I—"

Her phone buzzes, and I focus on the road as she responds to the text.

"Tracey had her baby last weekend," she says. "She just asked if I could tell our parents. Well, Ma. She doesn't care about our dad."

I have questions, but I don't ask them.

"You're probably wondering why Tracey wasn't at the wedding," Yvonne says. "She was invited, but she refuses to be in the same room as our father. When we were kids, she was the one who was always in trouble and couldn't maintain good grades. Turns out she has ADHD and needed help figuring out how to manage that, but she didn't get diagnosed until she was twenty-seven. She dropped out of university, and our parents were *not* happy, as I'm sure you can imagine."

"Yeah. I refused to apply to university."

"You did?" She's silent for a moment. "I guess in our parents' minds, there was only one path to success, and that involved a degree or two."

Exactly.

"You must have some higher education, though," she says. "To do what you do."

"I went back later. Just a two-year diploma. Didn't love it, but I survived."

"School was never your thing?"

"No. I'm not smart, and I was never very interested." I make a left-hand turn. "Just liked to draw rather than pay attention."

"I'm sure you're plenty smart."

"Not compared to my brothers."

My parents didn't make outright comparisons, but it was obvious that I was the one without brains. Nobody needed to say it out loud. Even I understood that much.

"Leo..."

"It's fine," I say. "I do okay."

Yvonne looks out the window. "I wasn't a very good sister to Tracey," she says, and I'm glad I'm not the topic of conversation anymore. I want to object to her words, but I just listen. "I couldn't understand why she wasn't, well, more like me. Why couldn't she hand in her assignments on time? Why did she cause our parents so much stress? I thought I understood everything, but I didn't." She sighs. "Sorry, I'm talking too much."

"It's fine," I repeat.

I like when you talk. I like learning about you. It's what I desired from the day I met her: to peel away her control and perfection. And now, when it's just the two of us, she doesn't avoid sharing the parts that she isn't proud of, but I won't let myself believe that means anything.

I pull into the busy IKEA parking lot and park far from the entrance.

"Thank you," she says, once I cut the engine. She places her hand over mine.

I swallow. The warmth of her skin is too much. I try to make some words come out of my mouth, but my throat isn't working properly.

"For what?" I croak at last.

"For being me a good friend and driving me around."

Yes. As a friend. That's how she sees me. I better not forget it.

I haven't been to IKEA in a long time, though I've ordered some stuff online on a couple of occasions. The store is so big, with too many people looking at furniture that they may or may not succeed in putting together. I don't know why anyone needs a plush heart with two hands coming out of it, but Yvonne holds it up and giggles. She tries to make the heart hug my bicep.

I pretend to be grumpier than I am.

She buys the stuff she needs, and I bring it to the car while she orders Swedish meatballs for us at the café.

"They serve poutine here," she says as she digs into her food. "I suspect it's just at the Canadian locations, right? I wonder how different the menu is at stores around the world." She sighs in contentment. "It's nice not to have last-minute dress fittings and arguments about flowers on the weekend. So much less stressful, even if I don't have a permanent place to live. I'm never planning a wedding again, that's for sure."

Once again, a few questions come to mind, but I don't ask them, and this time, she doesn't read my mind and ask them anyway.

But when her gaze catches mine, she smiles, and it's the cutest fucking thing. I swear she looks at me for a beat longer than usual—it feels like we're having a moment—but that's probably just my imagination.

"I'm working on my plans to enjoy my single life," she says when we're in the car, heading back to my parents' house. "Maybe I'll go out clubbing until two in the morning."

I can't imagine Yvonne as the clubbing type. Instead, I picture her dancing alone in her apartment, wearing...not much of anything. My mind often veers this way where she's concerned, but it doesn't help that we've spent the day at IKEA, like we're a normal couple.

"I'm kidding," she says.

"I figured."

"Yeah, it's not my thing." She laughs. "I'm excited about living by myself. That's an experience I've never had before. I'd also like to experience good sex."

If I'd been eating a meatball, I probably would have choked on it. Instead, I hit the brakes a split second later than I usually would as I approach a red light.

"Oh?" I say mildly.

"Not that I haven't enjoyed myself in the past, but it hasn't been incredible, you know?"

What I know is that if I had her in my bed—and I've thought about that more than I should—I would make very, *very* sure it was incredible for her.

Fortunately, I'm good at keeping my mouth shut.

I glance in her direction. She's looking out the passenger's window, and I can't make out her expression, but her cheeks are stained a light pink.

"And I was wondering," she says, "if maybe you could help me with that."

What?

What??

I must not have heard that right. It has to be wishful thinking.

"Like, I could go on an app," she continues, "but I'd feel more comfortable with someone I know already. Sure, it's a bit weird because you're Carl's cousin, but it's just sex."

Okay, I'm pretty sure I'm not hallucinating now, but...*what?*

"You think...I'd be good in bed?" I stammer.

"Am I wrong?"

I'm too shocked to reply.

"You're attracted to me, aren't you?" she says. "I've caught you looking at me a few times—"

"When?" Did she have an inkling of this before she ran away from her wedding?

"Earlier, when we were eating, for example."

If she only knew the half of it.

"So, what do you think?" she asks.

"No," I say immediately, before I can give into temptation. "Absolutely not."

My body screams at my words, but it would be a terrible idea. Because I *want*. I want more than taking her to bed a few times, and if I get a taste of her, I don't know how I'll ever be able to give her up. She's made it clear she just wants sex, but I want more than that.

I want to keep her.

And I know she's in no place for a relationship, plus I'm not the kind of guy she'd date anyway. Obviously, Carl wasn't right for her, but I still imagine her with someone a little more like him.

The next few minutes in the car are tenser than my shoulders after I've been sitting at a computer for twelve hours, but at least I did what I needed to do. I feel like I deserve a fucking medal, especially since it's been years since I had sex.

Finally, she breaks the silence. "I'm sorry I made things weird."

"It's fine." My words are clipped. I don't wish to talk about this.

But she keeps going. "Of course you're not interested in me like that. I was wrong. You're probably appalled by the idea, but you're too nice to admit you don't—"

"*Excuse me?*"

"I just misread your glances. My fault. Don't worry, you don't need to reassure me that many men would be happy to have me."

I can't take it anymore.

I turn into a plaza and park the car. I won't be able to concentrate on driving when I say my piece, and I'm about to tell Yvonne more than I ever intended for her to know.

Chapter 14

Yvonne

I FUCKED UP.

The only other time I made such a mess out of things? When I ran out of my wedding two weeks ago. But I don't regret that decision, and I guess that's what gave me the confidence to be bold.

To proposition my ex's cousin.

Leo has been kind to me, and now I'll never be able to see him again because it'll be too awkward. I don't know how I can come back from this. It was foolish to think he might want to get me naked, just because it's easy for me to picture his head between my thighs and he gave me...what? A couple of looks I apparently misinterpreted.

And now he's parked the car, and I'm half afraid he'll make me get out and walk. Why else would he have stopped?

Absolutely not.

The words ring in my ears.

The fact that he doesn't want me hurts more than it should. It reminds me of how unhappy I was with my body as a teenager. People would say nasty things about the bodies of amazing-looking pop stars and actresses, then wonder why teenage girls were insecure.

I've gained some confidence as an adult, but the wedding dress fittings didn't help. Being cheated on didn't help, either.

But I can't blame Leo for my insecurities.

I turn to him but can't meet his eyes. "Please, just drive me back to your parents' house, and you'll never have to see me again. I'm sorry I made you uncomfortable. I'm sorry—"

When he places a single finger to my lips, I shut up. His touch is distracting.

No, it's more than distracting; it's overwhelming. This sort of touch cannot be casual. With the tiniest movement, I could lick his finger.

I don't, but I can't help thinking of it, and the tension is unbearable.

He finally moves his hand, only to grasp my wrist.

"Yvonne," he says. "Listen."

I've made him listen to a lot in the last two weeks, and I can't say no. Even though there's something dangerous in his voice, something I've only heard one other time: when he thought I was a thief.

I shouldn't be excited by it, but I am.

"You think I said no because I don't want you."

"Yes?" I squeak. It comes out as a question. I realize there's something I don't understand here, and usually I hate uncertainties, but...

"Nothing," he bites out, "could be further from the truth."

My brain can barely comprehend his words. All my energy is focused on the hand around my wrist. That firm, deliberate touch—and what else he could do with those fingers.

"Look at me." He puts his other hand on my chin and tilts it up. "I need you to understand." He pauses, and the wait for his next words is excruciating. "I want to toss you in the back seat and fuck you right here, right now."

Oh my God.

I inhale swiftly. My entire body is vibrating with need.

"When I was in the shower this morning," he says, "I had my hand on my cock and you on my mind. I imagined fucking you from behind...and when I stopped, you begged me for more. My thoughts about you—they're filthy."

"And what? I'm too much of a good girl for that?"

He hisses out a breath, like I'm testing his willpower. I'm not sure I've ever done that to someone before, and it's invigorating.

"You think I can't handle it?" I ask.

His grasp tightens on my wrist. His other hand is still under my chin. "I think this would be a very, very bad idea."

"Because of Carl?"

God, why did I have to date that cheating bastard? I'm not sure I've ever resented him so much before—and that's saying something.

"Trust me," Leo says. "It's not a good idea."

"Okay, I'll find someone else."

Who *am* I right now?

His nostrils flare, and he pulls me closer, his face just a few inches from mine, and all I can think is that I was very, *very* wrong about my type. He's the sexiest fucking man I've ever seen, and he's about two seconds away from kissing me.

Do it.

There's a pulse between my legs, and it feels like it's in time with his heavy breaths. His lips are parted, and he's so, so close...

It's too intense to look at his face, at those piercing dark eyes, so I glance at his arm instead, but that's no better. Black ink peeks out from under his T-shirt, and I want to remove that shirt and see what art he's put permanently on his body. I want to feel his muscles bunch beneath my fingertips.

"Leo," I whisper.

When he presses his mouth to mine, my eyes flutter closed. *Oh. My. God.*

He's kissing me, and it's incredible. The first few seconds are almost savage, but then his lips gentle as he explores me. I kiss him back and sink into the moment. It feels right and oh-so-wrong at the same time, and my toes curl in my shoes. I've certainly never had a make-out session like this before. I've never been so consumed by desperation. I need—

He releases me with a growl.

"Fuck," he says. "We can't..."

I'm in such a daze that I barely notice him backing out of the parking spot and pulling onto the street. Nothing more is going to happen, and I feel a keen sense of disappointment

But that kiss has changed me. Because there is absolutely no doubt now that he wants me.

And I want him more than I thought possible.

Lynne and Howie aren't around, thankfully. I'm used to smiling and making polite conversation, but after what happened with their son, I don't know if I'd be able to do that.

I go to my temporary room, where I set up my plant stand. When I'm an old plant lady, I'll probably still be thinking about that time Leo Mok kissed him.

Part of the thrill? Learning that he sees me in a completely different way from how everyone else sees me, and that knowledge has expanded my world.

My parents liked that I was obedient and made their lives easy.

Carl saw me as good wife material, I guess.

But Leo...

I pick up the frame with Francine's portrait. The cheerful whimsy of the drawing seems at odds with who he was in the car, but I like that there are different sides to him.

I wonder if he's ever drawn me?

No. I can't keep dwelling on this, but I also can't seem to think of anything else.

I lie back on the bed and call Shauna.

"Hey!" she says. "What's up?"

"I propositioned him." I'm unable to deal with pleasantries at the moment. "Leo, I mean."

"And? Was it good?"

"You don't know if he said yes."

She scoffs. "Yeah, but he should have."

"Well, he said no. He thought it would be a bad idea, but he really, really wanted to. When I told him I'd find someone else, if he wasn't willing to show me what good sex was like, he kissed me."

Shauna shrieks. "I can't believe you did that."

"Me, neither." I shut my eyes as I remember how he touched me. "But nothing more happened. He feels loyal to Carl, I guess, even though they're not close."

"How noble of him."

I still don't fully understand why he turned me down. I think there's something more going on, but what?

"So, are you going to find someone else?" she asks.

"Not right now." I'd just compare every man to Leo. Besides... "I should focus on getting an apartment. I won't think about it until I've signed a lease."

"That's okay. You've got time. Hey, you want to come over, maybe bring your wedding dress? I'm itching to get started on making you the hottest zombie bride."

"I'm not sure you can make a *hot* zombie bride costume."

"Is that a challenge?"

An hour later, I'm on a bus, my wedding dress in a garbage bag on my lap.

Seeing Shauna is a good distraction, and there's something satisfying about ripping up the bottom of my bridal gown.

"What's that stain?" she asks.

"Chocolate ice cream. I had ice cream with Leo in the park." My cheeks heat just from saying his name.

"We'll cover it in blood. No one will notice."

I don't mention him again, but it's hard not to think of Leo when I'm in his old bedroom, trying to fall asleep. I swear I can still feel his fingers on my mouth and on my wrist. Based on that kiss, anything more would be incendiary, and if he kissed his way down my body...

Fuck.

I've never felt lust like this before.

But then I wonder if it was all a mistake. How am I supposed to hang out with him, now that I know he fantasizes about me?

It feels like his desires are very much about me, Yvonne Siu, not just some random woman he finds rather attractive. I might have only started spending time with him two weeks ago, but he knows me reasonably well—and not the part of myself who pastes on a smile and goes along with what other people want.

I wonder what, exactly, I do in his fantasies. How shameless am I?

Being wanted like this...it's exhilarating and frustrating at the same time. I desperately—*desperately*—yearn for more, though I have to respect his wishes. He said no, and I'll find someone else eventually.

But for now...

I take out my very, very quiet vibrator.

Chapter 15

Leo

"Party too much on the weekend?" Dinesh asks with a waggle of his eyebrows as I pour myself an extra-large coffee.

I probably look tired, but it's not because I partied. No, after driving Yvonne back to my parents' house, I spent most of the long weekend in my apartment. It took a few hours to finish up the latest commission, but other than that, I was distracted by thoughts of her. When I tried to start a new show, I could barely focus enough to figure out what was going on.

Yvonne asked me to sleep with her. She asked me to show her what good sex is like because apparently, she wasn't having that with her ex.

Never in my wildest dreams did I think this would happen.

After I told her that I wanted to fuck her in the back seat, I kissed her. She melted against me and leaned into my touch, but somehow, I managed to end it.

It would have been easy to say that I was taking her back to my place...and wouldn't let her leave until Monday morning. But it would have been a terrible idea. I already went too far—I kissed my cousin's ex in a busy parking lot—yet knowing that didn't stop me from thinking about it all weekend. From staying up until four last night because I couldn't get her out of my brain.

Dinesh responds to my silence with a laugh. "Sure seems like you did."

I return to my desk, where Pablo shoots me a look of concern.

"You okay?" he asks.

"I'm good," I say.

As in, I don't want to talk about it, and he gets the message.

When I was a kid, the Tuesday after Labor Day meant returning to school. It was a day I dreaded. But since I no longer get two months off in the summer, it's just another week at the office, and my mind is already skipping forward to the weekend.

Will Yvonne ask to see me again?

And will I be too weak to say no?

I hear from Yvonne on Friday, but she doesn't ask me to drive her to IKEA or meet her for brunch. Nor does she ask me to sleep with her. No, she sends me a picture of a leaf in a jar of water. It looks like a cutting from Francine.

> YVONNE: Do you make pottery?

> YVONNE: I mean, since you're artsy, I figured you might.

> YVONNE: Maybe I'll take it up one day so I can make pots for my plants.

It feels like Saturday's conversation and kiss never even happened, but she must think of it every now and then, right? She must think of it at least one-tenth as much as I do.

ME: I don't

ME: How did you get into plants?

YVONNE: For my birthday one year, my old boss got me a spider plant. I kinda liked looking after it, but I could see I wasn't doing a great job. The leaves were turning yellow. So I started reading up on houseplants and…IDK. It was fun but didn't demand too much from me.

YVONNE: Can't wait to be an old lady with a house full of plants. No cats. Just plants.

I hesitate before asking my next question.

ME: Any plans for the weekend?

YVONNE: Looking at apartments tomorrow.

And that's all. She doesn't ask to see me, like she has the last two weekends, and it's more of a blow then it should be.

I toss my phone aside and turn on the TV. I scroll through Netflix, unable to settle on anything because Yvonne's still on my mind. Even though it's been almost a week, I keep wondering what would have happened if I'd slipped my hand under her shirt. Would she have moaned when I cupped her breasts? I shouldn't think about this again and again, yet I can't help it.

When my phone buzzes again, I pounce on it, convinced it's her.

But it's my mom, saying she has a bunch of stuff for me to pick up tomorrow.

"I'm cleaning out the basement," Mom says as she ushers me down the stairs.

My parents finished the basement when I was a kid. Extra space for us to play in, and later, Max had his bedroom down here so all four of us could have our own rooms. Now, it's mainly used for storage.

Nobody else is home. Dad often goes grocery shopping on Saturday mornings.

"These are yours." Mom gestures at two cardboard boxes. "Mostly from school."

"I don't want them."

"Ah, Leo." She gives me a look. "You should at least see what's there. I didn't think you'd want most of it, but you might like to keep a few items."

I'm surprised this stuff still exists. I'd assumed my school things were thrown out years ago. After all, I'm the third child, and usually by the time families get to kid number three, they're less interested in keeping mementos. Besides, it's not like I had impressive test results or awards.

"Fine." I pick up both boxes and take them to the living room. My mom leaves me alone as I open them up.

The first thing I find is a story I wrote in grade three.

Well, saying I did any writing would be generous. There are a few poorly spelled words, but it's mainly pictures in pencil crayon.

Next, a science test on which I miraculously got an A.

A title page that I drew for a unit in French class.

Two sheets of graph paper that look like they were torn out of a notebook I would have used for math. There are large bubble numbers that have been turned into cape-wearing superheroes.

A map of Canada with "Saskatchewan" spelled wrong.

At least, I think it's spelled wrong. I'm not entirely sure.

I set a few things aside—I want evidence that I spent all those years in school, I guess—but put most of it back in the boxes.

Mom comes in with some tea for me. "You're finished? Already?"

When I nod, she sits down beside me. The two of us aren't the talkers in the family. When it's just us, there are bound to be more than a few silences. Usually, I wouldn't mind, but now, I feel the need to fill the silence.

"I can't believe you kept all that," I say.

"Ah, why not?"

Rather than use my piss-poor communication skills, I stay quiet.

"You know," she says, "I wish we had seen more than one possible path for you. Sometimes, it was—how do you say? Like we were trying to fit a square peg into a round hole. I understand that now. You did well, Leo."

I merely nod again, but inside, I feel something loosen in my chest.

I know I'm lucky. My parents weren't hard-asses to the degree of some of my classmates. They didn't throw out my comics and tell me to only read proper books. They didn't expect me to get an A-plus in every subject, though yes, they were disappointed in my marks.

I think of Yvonne and her sister.

Mom smiles and pats my hand, and then we stand up at the same time. I guess we've decided this is enough for one day.

"Are you going to throw the rest of it out?" I gesture to the boxes.

"No, there are a few things I'll keep. I'll add them to the other box I have—stuff that isn't schoolwork." She pauses. "Yvonne is looking at apartments, in case you were wondering."

"Yes, she told me."

Mom studies me, and although my face isn't terribly expressive, she's my mother—and I fear she can see everything on it. Can she tell that I kissed my cousin's ex? Despite this nice moment we've shared today, I don't think she'd approve.

The front door opens, and she heads into the hall. When I hear Yvonne's voice and not my father's, my body smiles and tenses at the same time. I long to see her, but it feels too dangerous. It'll be suspicious if I don't say hello, though, so I walk toward the door.

"Hi...Leo," she stammers, and Mom gives me an odd look.

Shit.

"Just picking up some stuff," I say. "How were the apartments?"

But I can tell from the way she's carrying herself that it didn't go well. Or maybe she's just ruffled by my presence.

She shakes her head. "The first one was a joke. No wonder the price seemed too good to be true—it was. I don't know much about buildings, but it looked unsafe, like something would fall down at any minute, and the toilet was in the kitchen. *In* the kitchen—well, what passed for a kitchen. No oven or stove."

"The second one?" Mom asks.

"When I arrived, they told me it had just been taken."

"It's okay," Mom says. "You will stay here until you find something decent. No need to rush and end up somewhere unsafe."

I appreciate that my parents have been kind to Yvonne, but the longer she stays here, the longer I have to see her when I visit...and pretend I didn't kiss her. I've studiously avoided looking at her lips, but now, I stare at her hands and imagine them on my skin.

"You're only supposed to spend thirty percent of your gross income on rent," Yvonne says. I'm not sure what "gross" means—is that before or after tax? "But I don't see how that's possible for most people in Toronto these days."

"Is there anything in your building, Leo?" Mom asks.

I bend down to put on my shoes. "I'll check."

I don't know how I'd survive Yvonne living so close to me, but yeah, I'll look into it.

When I exit the house and start driving home, I finally feel like I can breathe again, but then I remember that we kissed in my car last Saturday. I was sitting in this very seat when I first felt her lips on mine.

"Fuck me," I mutter.

Chapter 16

Yvonne

I shouldn't have propositioned Leo. Everything is weird now. He wouldn't look at me earlier, and I could feel Lynne wanting to ask what was going on.

And I don't have time to think about that. I promised Tracey that I'd tell our mom about the baby, and I have to do it today.

Yesterday evening, I spent half an hour staring at my phone, trying to get up the nerve to make that call, but I couldn't.

You know your eldest daughter, the one you don't talk to anymore? She had a baby boy.

Since I couldn't say it over the phone—and I felt like it deserved more than a text—I told Ma that I'd visit this afternoon.

Lynne insists I take her car, and I drive slowly, not looking forward to arriving at my parents' house. At least my dad won't be home. Not that he's talking to me at the moment anyway.

I park in the driveway and walk to the door. Ma opens it before I get there.

"Why are you dawdling?" she asks.

I don't answer. Once I'm inside, I lead her to the front room. We sit side by side on the couch, and I take a moment to compose myself. I'm worried about a shoot-the-messenger situation. Not that this is bad news—no, it's very good news—but I'm afraid she'll be angry that she's hearing it from me, rather than my sister.

"Ma." I swallow. "Tracey had a baby. You're a grandmother."

There's no anger. I see only regret on my mother's face—and that's easy for me to recognize. I'm intimately familiar with regret right now. Leo, Carl...

"You want to see a picture?" I ask. Tracey told me this was okay.

Ma nods.

I pull out my phone and bring up a photo of Tracey and the baby in the hospital, then another picture of them at home.

She peers at the screen. "Boy or girl?"

"Boy."

Ma smiles. Is she glad it's a boy instead of a girl? Or is she just glad to learn anything about her grandchild?

"What's his name?" she asks.

"Last I heard, they hadn't decided on a name. He was born two weeks ago."

"Two weeks!"

"I didn't know she was pregnant, either. Not until the week before."

"I should go to Tracey. She needs someone to look after her."

"Rob is looking after her."

"Men don't know about these things," Ma says dismissively. "What's her address?"

And this is why Tracey wanted me to break the news. Talking to Ma can use up a lot of energy, and she needs that energy for other things.

"Rob will take good care of her," I say gently.

"Your dad didn't. I was all alone in a new country, no family—"

"Ma. Listen."

"Is she still taking those pills? Is she breastfeeding? Will—"

"I don't know," I interrupt, "but I'm sure she discussed it with her doctor. I don't know what's recommended."

Tracey takes medication for ADHD—at least, she did a few years ago. I don't think our mom approves, and our dad definitely doesn't.

Ma huffs, but then she takes my phone, and her face softens. "Fine. I understand why you won't tell me where she lives. Seeing me will be stressful for her, and that won't be good."

I stare at my mom, surprised she's actually admitting that.

"But maybe I can buy a present? Cook her some food? Ask if she will accept that from me, and then you can bring it next weekend, yes?"

I nod.

"I still remember what she likes." Ma smiles sadly and wipes her eyes.

Is my mother crying? Completely thrown by this development, I pat her shoulder, but I don't say anything.

This past month has been...a lot.

After I walk out of my parents' house, I get into the Camry and text Tracey.

I'm surprised—but pleased—when my sister answers right away and asks me to come over. I assure her that I'm up to date with my vaccinations and I'm feeling well. I also tell her that I'll wear a mask, just in case. The last thing I want to do is get my newborn nephew sick.

It's a twenty-minute drive to my sister's apartment, and as I walk up to the door, mask in place, I think of the last time I was here, in my wedding dress.

When I knock on the door, a voice shouts, "It's unlocked!"

Inside, I take off my shoes and find Tracey sitting on the couch, nursing the baby.

"Hey," she says to me with a tired smile.

I sit beside her. "How are you?"

"As well as can be expected, considering I pushed ten pounds out of my body not all that long ago."

"Ten pounds!" I study the baby in her arms. I haven't spent a ton of time around newborns, so I can't tell if he's bigger than the average two-week-old.

"The babies in Rob's family are always big. Lucky me."

"I told Ma that he'd take care of you, but she doesn't believe men are capable of that."

Tracey rolls her eyes, and for a split second, I see her as a rebellious teenager again.

"I'm sorry I made you break the news to her," she says. "Some part of me just wanted her to know."

"It's fine. It wasn't as bad as I expected, and at least it made her forget about my drama." I hesitate. "Do you think you'll ever have a relationship with them again? I'm not saying you should." I'm prepared for her to get defensive. "Just asking."

She looks down at her son. "Maybe, but only Ma. If she divorces him—"

I bark out a laugh, and the baby starts fussing, but Tracey quickly gets him settled.

"You really think she'd do that?" I ask.

"No, but she should. I think a lot of her expectations of us...sure, some of it was her, but I'm pretty sure most of it was him. She just didn't want him to be angry."

"Really?"

"I know your childhood was different from mine," she says ruefully. "Sometimes, I'd go to Ma with an issue—if it was something that I couldn't hide—and she'd promise to deal with it as long as he didn't find out. When I was grounded, she'd sneak me things. I don't think she'd be near as judgmental if she wasn't worrying about what he'd say."

Perhaps Tracey is right.

"For now, I'll accept a gift, but only if it's through you. I'm not ready to see her."

I glance down at my nephew. He's asleep, and Tracey has pulled him off her breast. She smooths his wispy hair with her fingers, then all of a sudden, a look of terror appears on her face.

"How did I think I could handle this?" she whispers. "Being a mother—it's too much."

"You'll do great." I pat her hand. "You won't be perfect—nobody can—but that's okay."

"Is it?"

"You never expected perfection from yourself before."

"I have a *baby* now. It's different. And I can't even figure out what to name him. We just call him 'Baby.'"

"Who says that can't be a name?" I say lightly. "*Dirty Dancing*, remember? Okay, maybe it was a nickname, but still."

She chuckles, and that feels like an accomplishment.

"If you decide to see Ma," I say, "I can be there."

"I can't ask you to mediate. You spent so much of your childhood trying to do that."

Yeah, without much success. I didn't understand why Tracey couldn't just *behave*, like I did, especially since she was the big sister.

But I understand much better than I did back then. When I was a kid, I knew people were different, but I didn't understand how fundamentally different people could be.

"Just the first time," I say. "So that there's someone to lead her out, if necessary."

"Okay." She touches my shoulder. "I don't want to go a year without seeing you again."

"Same." I smile at her and remember how she'd let me sneak into her bed after I'd read a scary book and was too frightened to be alone. We might not have been the closest of siblings, but she was a good big sister. "And really, I think you'll be a great mother."

She hands the baby to me. "You can hold him while I go to the washroom. Don't try to put him in the bassinet—he doesn't like it."

My sister gets up, and I gently rock my nephew. I don't speak to him, just admire his impossibly tiny hands and fingernails, his little legs in his green onesie, his tuft of dark hair. I'm happy to hold him, but I wouldn't want to be responsible for him 24/7.

Yes, meeting my nephew has reassured me that I'm right about my future: I don't want kids of my own.

"Sorry, I was out longer than expected," I say as I hang the car keys on the rack in the kitchen. I texted Lynne before going to my sister's, just to make sure she didn't need the car. Sometimes I'm unsure of what I should tell Lynne and Howie about my daily activities. Yes, I'm an adult, but I'm living with them for now.

"It's no problem." Lynne opens the dishwasher.

"Here, let me help you."

She tries to shoo me away, but she can no longer use the excuse that I don't know where everything goes. In my weeks here, I've learned where all the dishes belong.

We work in silence for a couple of minutes, and when everything has been put away, she says, "Are you okay? You seem a bit..." She makes a gesture with her hand.

"Seeing my mom is draining, that's all."

She's quiet for a moment. "Are you having problems with my son?"

"What?! I have no idea what you're talking about." I don't make a show of asking which son, though. I assume she means the one I saw when I returned from apartment-hunting. Maybe she noticed the weird tension between me and Leo.

She gives me a look. "Did you have a fight?"

"No."

I wonder how horrified she'd be if she knew I made out with him. I've been shedding my people-pleasing ways, but I respect Lynne, and I want to have her respect in return. I want to continue to be on good terms when I'm finally able to move out.

Fortunately, she doesn't say anything more.

The following week is a normal week—at least, as far as my new normal goes. I commute. I work. I have dinner with Lynne and Howie. I fail to find a new apartment. I text Shauna. I get a picture of my new baby nephew, but still no name. I talk to Francine and tell her that she's looking well.

One evening, I open up Instagram for the first time in weeks. I never posted a lot, but I'd share the occasional pictures of my perfect-looking life. A year ago, I was so certain of what my future would entail...and then it lost its appeal.

I put down my phone and look at the drawing of Francine in its simple frame. It makes me think of Leo. As the first person who saw me after I ran out of the church, he's has been an important part of my new life, and it's weird that I've barely talked to him in over a week, aside from that very brief—and awkward—meeting in the front hall.

I miss him.

On Friday night, a weekend without plans stretches before me, and I send him a text, asking if he wants to try a new ramen restaurant. I won't mention the kiss or what I said in his car, even if I think about it when I can't sleep.

We can go back to the way things used to be, right?

Or maybe you can never go back.

Chapter 17

Leo

That kiss continues to ruin me, and at work, Dinesh makes another crack about how I've been partying a lot lately.

Ha. No. I just haven't been sleeping.

When Yvonne asks if I want to hang out, I say yes. I used all my willpower to refuse sex; I can't deny her anything else.

"Hi, Leo!" she says brightly when we meet outside of the restaurant. "How was your week?"

"Fine," I reply in a clipped voice, as I try not to admire everything about her. "I checked to see if there are any apartments for rent in my building. Only a two-bedroom." I was relieved—and disappointed—to learn there was nothing suitable. I can't imagine she wants the expense of two bedrooms.

She places her hand on my arm. "Thank you."

I freeze at the contact, and she immediately withdraws.

"Sorry," she says.

She doesn't mention what happened two Saturdays ago, but I know it's on her mind.

Goddammit.

Inside the restaurant, the only seats left are at the counter by the window, which is unfortunate. Not just because the sun is bright; the seating is rather cramped, and Yvonne's knee is only an inch from mine.

I try to read the menu on my phone, but I can barely focus, and when the waitress comes around, I just order the pork shoyu, which I'm pretty sure is what I had the last time I went out for ramen. Yvonne gets the black garlic broth.

After we place our orders, there's an awkward silence, but Yvonne quickly fills it, talking about her visits with her mother and sister. She shows me a picture of her little nephew.

I could get used to this. Seeing her every weekend. Listening to the mundane and not-so-mundane details of her life—that would be enough, right?

"Why are you shaking your head?" she asks.

"There was a fly," I lie.

"Am I talking too much?

"No."

When Yvonne shifts on her stool, her knee knocks against mine, and I exhale unsteadily.

"Once again," she says. "I'm sorry about the other weekend. It was presumptuous—"

I hold up a hand. I'm happy for her to do most of the talking, but not about this. Not right now. If she says any more, I might kiss her to shut her up.

Maybe I should have taken her home with me. Maybe, if I knew how it feels to have her body underneath mine, I could stop wondering. I could get it out of my system. I could have a proper night's sleep.

I'm not foolish enough to think that one time would be enough. But maybe two or three—or ten—would do?

Like she said, nobody else would have to know. And I'd be doing her a favor—showing her what sex can be like so she won't settle next time.

Yeah, that's me. Totally selfless.

It's less awkward once our food arrives. That is, until Yvonne starts making sounds of pure pleasure as she consumes her noodles and broth.

"It's so rich," she says.

I try to focus on my own noodles, but it's impossible to ignore the woman next to me.

At the end of the meal, I grab the bill before she can, and she lets me pay with only a little argument.

"It's such a beautiful day," she says as we walk outside, "though this isn't the best place to enjoy it. The Scarborough Bluffs aren't far from here, right? Maybe we could go there."

I grunt.

"We don't have to—"

"We'll go," I say, rather than try to communicate what I'm feeling.

When we're in my car, she pulls out her phone for directions. My hands tighten on the steering wheel, and I regret agreeing to see her today. Because we kissed...right here. I was parked in front of a different plaza, but still.

It's not a long drive, but it feels long with her sitting next to me. By the time we exit the car and look out at Lake Ontario, the sun is hiding behind some clouds. I hope she won't want to go for a walk; I'm not sure I could survive it in her company.

Yvonne's hair is loose, and the wind off the lake whips it around. "It's so nice to do something spontaneous." She tips her head back.

Then two things happen at once: the sun peeks out from behind the clouds, and she smiles. The way her face captures the light and shadows...it takes my breath away, even more than usual.

Fuck it. I can't handle this anymore. How can I hold back when I know she wants it?

I pull her toward me and kiss her. She melts against me in the sunshine. I slip one hand into her hair, securing it against the wind as her mouth moves with mine. Since we're not in the car this time, there's no console between us, and I can feel her breasts against my chest. When she moans, it's way more erotic than when she tasted the black garlic broth.

"Come home with me," I say urgently.

"I thought—"

"I changed my mind."

"Even though I'm Carl's ex?"

"Yes." Because I'm not sure how I can survive otherwise. I need to know what it's like with her. "But I have a few rules."

I haven't figured out what they are yet, but I know I'll require something. Something to keep this from getting completely out of hand until I've gotten her out of my system.

She nods. "I won't expect to stay the night, don't worry."

"It's not just that." I pause. "I don't want you in my bed at all."

"I thought you asked me to come home with—"

"There are other places to have sex." A collage of images fills my mind.

She's quiet, and I wonder if I've shocked her.

"Okay," she says at last. "I agree to your rules."

In one sense, it feels like we're being very adult about this, discussing everything beforehand. Setting boundaries.

On the other hand...

I want to touch her so badly that I couldn't even watch the sun touch her face without kissing her. It was easier before, when I thought she had no interest.

But this is good for her, right?

She wants to experience great sex, and I'll treat her well. Even if I'm a bit out of practice, I know I can satisfy her.

And by refusing to do it in my bed, I'm making sure I won't get any romantic ideas. No falling asleep together and cuddling. It'll just be sex. I might not be the smart one, and that rule might have come out of my mouth before I gave it much thought, but I think it's a solid plan.

I press a bruising kiss to her lips. I can't wait until I can unbutton her jeans and feel her moisture on my fingers, but that will have to wait until we're in my apartment.

I grab her hand. "Let's go."

Chapter 18

Yvonne

WHEN I TOOK THE bus to meet Leo for lunch, I didn't expect him to change his mind, but that doesn't mean this isn't a welcome development. Before I left, I slipped a few condoms in my purse, just in case.

He doesn't speak on the drive to his apartment, and he doesn't sneak glances at me. No, his gaze is focused on the road, and unlike the other times I've been in the car with him, he speeds. Just a little.

Me, on the other hand? I can't keep myself from looking over, and I can't stop the pulse between my legs.

"Are you afraid of snakes?" he asks suddenly.

"What?" I yelp. "Do you have a python?" I swear he said he didn't have any pets, back when I asked him to look after Francine.

His lips twitch, and I itch to touch them. To kiss them.

"No," he says. "I did ask my parents for one when I was seven, but...no."

I'm lost.

His left hand leaves the steering wheel for a split second, and he pulls up his right sleeve.

Oh.

I examine the reptile that coils around his bicep. I wish I could trace it with my finger. "It's not like that's a real snake."

"It caused a problem once in the past." He doesn't elaborate.

"What does the tattoo mean?"

"I'm not a very deep guy. I was nineteen and thought it was cool."

Yeah, Leo and I are rather different. When I was nineteen, I certainly never did something simply because it looked cool.

But it doesn't matter how different we are. I'm not planning a future with him; I just want to fuck.

I inhale sharply at the thought.

"Change your mind?" he asks.

"No. I'm sure."

He shoots me a quick glance, and it's searing.

Traffic isn't bad, but it's still far too long before he turns into the underground parking garage of a high-rise. We wait for the elevator, side by side. I don't dare touch him, afraid I won't be able to stop if I start. I used to have pretty good self-control, but that was before I blew apart my life.

We're silent until the doors open. This elevator is going down, not up.

"Fuck," Leo whispers, and I try not to feel pleased. He's eager to get his hands on *me*.

Finally, we're in the elevator...and then we're on his floor...and he's opening a door...

The first thing I notice in his apartment? The bed. It's a studio apartment, so there isn't a separate bedroom. The bed is right *there*, but we're not going to use it. I'm not certain why he has this rule, but I can't think straight right now. The most important thing is that he's going to fuck me.

I toe off my shoes, and he does the same. We stand right inside the door, staring at each other. I'm eager to touch him, but how does one start something like this?

"You good?" he asks.

"Yeah."

As soon as I say it, he whips my shirt over my head and drops it to the floor. His own shirt follows. Then he backs me against the wall and kisses me.

This time, I can feel his skin against mine.

And this time, I know a kiss won't be where it ends. We're all alone. No one will see us, and I can take what I want.

I run my hands over his solid arm muscles, then over his chest and belly. Since Leo is just a few inches taller than me, there isn't a big height different to navigate. When I lick the snake with my tongue, he hisses out a breath and slides his leg between mine. I rock myself against his erection, and he groans.

I'm not a physical person—I'm usually very much in my mind—but today, I just want to enjoy my body. And his.

He pulls me away from the wall and spins me around. His fingers work on the button of my jeans, then the zipper. My pussy clenches, desperate for his touch.

But when he slides his hand inside my panties, I stiffen.

"No?" he asks.

When I don't respond, he starts to withdraw, but I put my hand over his wrist to keep him there. I want him to touch me. It's just...the closet door is a mirror, and I can see myself, topless. And there's a man behind me, a man I'm not dating, who has one hand in my pants while the other fondles my breast.

I've never insisted on sex with the lights out—okay, maybe I did the first few times, when I was twenty-one—but I don't particularly enjoy looking at myself. When you're naked, you can't hide your flaws. They're on display.

Leo doesn't say anything, just holds my gaze in the mirror, and there's something uncomfortable about that, but then he shuts his eyes and kisses the side of my neck.

I watch the woman in the mirror gasp.

I watch her jerk when his hand dips lower.

He pushes his finger inside, and *oh my God*, that feels amazing. When he adds a second finger, I tip my head back.

But I don't close my eyes.

For some reason, I enjoy watching myself be pleasured. Maybe because I feel like I'm watching some other woman, who's bold and wanton.

I clench around Leo's fingers.

He removes his hand, slides down my underwear and pants in one smooth motion, and kneels between my legs. He places my hands on his head. I lean back against the wall as he licks me, circling his tongue around my clit.

"It takes me a long time...to come," I tell him. "My legs...will collapse...before then."

He stands up, and the next thing I know, he's brought over a chair. He sets it in front of the mirror and gestures for me to take a seat.

I do, and he kneels between my legs once more and separates my knees.

"Really," I say, "it takes me a long time. I don't expect you to—"

His head jerks up, and he gives me a devastating look.

And then he goes right back to eating me out.

I groan as I stare at us in the mirror. The sight of him between my legs, the flex of his back muscles under golden skin...it really is erotic. He has tattoos on his back, but I can't focus on what they are, not now. I just watch us. Together.

Pressure builds slowly, but steadily, within me. He slips a finger inside me. I look down at his face—his eyes are closed, as if he's savoring my taste—then I glance back at the mirror and gasp.

I still can't get used to the fact that this is *me*.

I'm gripping the back of his head. My legs are spread wide. I raise one hand to squeeze my breast, tweak my nipple.

I feel like I'm performing for someone.

Then he licks me just right, and I watch myself come apart, the orgasm more powerful than any I've given myself.

He continues to touch me as my climax ebbs, until I tap him on the shoulder.

"I have a condom in my purse," I say.

We both stand up at the same time. Our lips are so close, and I need to kiss him before I do anything else. I set my mouth to his. He devours me, but when I unzip his pants and slide my hand inside, he turns away, as though it's too much for him.

He's hot and hard, and I want him inside me so badly.

"Yvonne..."

I let go of him, and he shucks off the rest of his clothes while I grab the condom. He looks amazing—and unlike any man I've been with before. He's not lean or chiseled, but there's something about him that radiates strength, and the intensity of his gaze on me...

I hand him the packet. He rolls the condom over his erection, then turns the chair and positions me so I'm bent over the back of it. I tense in anticipation as he moves behind me and rubs the head of his cock over my entrance. Over my copious wetness.

"Please," I whisper.

I look at the mirror, watching him handle his cock. He rubs the tip over me again, and just as I'm opening my mouth to beg him once more, he eases himself inside. I moan.

This is what I want. What I need.

I clutch the back of the chair as he begins moving within me, my head tipped to the side so I can watch us. His hands on my hips, his body thrusting against mine. Four weeks ago, I was supposed to get married...and now my ex-fiancé's cousin is fucking me, and it feels amazing.

I'm a bad, bad girl, and I've never been one of those before.

My legs wobble, and I grip the chair harder, but it's not enough. I straighten up, and his cock slides out of me. I gesture for him to take a seat on the chair. Then I wrap my hand around his cock and lower myself onto him.

My back is to the mirror now. I can't watch us like I could before, but I can see the pleasure my body gives him, written all over his face as I ride him. There's a notch between his eyebrows, and his lips are parted, and he's looking at me like I'm all that fucking matters in the world right now—and it doesn't make me want to hide.

I feel *free*.

I slide a hand over his chest, and he licks his thumb and drops his hand between my legs.

"Can you come again?" he asks.

"Yes." After I come once, the second time is a little easier.

He circles my clit, and I exhale shakily. God, he's good. It feels like he's so attuned to me. With one hand on his head and the other on his neck, I kiss him, and it feels decadent. I smile against his lips, and then I slip my tongue inside his mouth. He makes a strangled sound.

"Yvonne..."

I keep kissing him, and I ride him faster, chasing my release—and his. His hips move in time with mine, and it's overwhelming and *good*. I reach my peak a second before he does; he wrenches his mouth away from mine and growls.

"*Fuck*," he bites out.

We stay there for a moment, suspended in time, but I know this can't last. He's wearing a condom; I have to get off him before he softens inside me, and I deflate at the thought.

I stand up on weak legs, and before I can think about what to do next, he spins me around and sits me down on his knee so that I'm facing the mirror.

He buries two fingers in my pussy.

I'm used to men losing interest in my body once they've gotten off, but apparently, Leo is different. My legs are shaking, but I still want—and I can take. I ride his hand.

"So fucking sexy," he murmurs.

Oh God. It won't be much longer.

His thumb brushes my clit, and I roll my hips...and that's it. I'm done.

I convulse on his lap.

He eases his hand out of me, and I turn around, sitting so I can face him. As I watch him slide those fingers that were just inside me into his mouth, I feel a twitch of desire, but...no. I'm spent.

"Where's the washroom?" I ask.

He points me in the right direction, and once I close the door, I cover my face with my hands and giggle.

That was incredible, the sex I always hoped was possible for me.

And it was just sex.

Is that the key? Doing it outside of a relationship, without any other expectations?

After I finish washing up, I head back to the front hall. I'm completely nude—and I don't feel self-conscious about it.

Leo throws out the condom, then puts on his boxers and returns to the chair. I sit on his lap again. Even if I'm not allowed on his bed, I'm glad I can touch him afterward. It feels necessary.

"Hey," I say.

"Hey."

I trace the snake that curls around his bicep.

"Thank you," I say to the snake's head.

"You don't need to thank me for sex. It's not like I was doing you a favor. I enjoyed myself...a lot."

"Still. Thank you. For making it so good. It was exactly what I wanted." Yet in some ways, not at all what I'd expected. Like, I enjoyed watching us in the mirror. Do I have an exhibitionist streak? What does that mean?

I smile at Leo, and he smiles back, and there's something soft and unguarded that I've never seen in his expression before. It causes a strange warmth in my chest.

"We should do that again sometime," I say.

"Yeah. We should."

He presses a languid kiss to my lips, and I just want to smile forever.

We sit on the chair for a few more minutes before getting dressed, then Leo drives me back to his parents' house.

Thank God Lynne and Howie aren't home—they're visiting friends. I don't know how I'd be able to look them in the eye.

I do little for the rest of the day. I half-heartedly search for apartments, waste time on a houseplants forum, and make myself a simple dinner.

The sex I had with Leo is never far from mind. I feel like it's opened up a world of possibility, and not just in the bedroom—or on a chair. I'm not sure how else to explain it.

As I'm getting ready for bed, my gaze lands on the picture of Francine. I run my finger over the lines that Leo used to capture her, imagine his hands moving over the tablet, and I wonder where this is going.

I don't know when I'll see him again.

I don't know if he's sleeping with other people.

But I do know that no one can find out about this, with the exception of Shauna. I might tell her, but otherwise, I can't say a word.

The fact that I have a dirty little secret? It's exciting, but an odd melancholy hits me, too.

Well, I'm sure that will disappear soon.

Chapter 19

Leo

HOURS LATER, I CAN still taste Yvonne on my lips. I can still feel the weight of her in my lap, the clench of her around my cock.

It was fucking heaven.

Nobody had ever made her feel quite like I did. That much was clear, and it was certainly a boost to my pride. But how could anyone see her orgasm and not want to make it happen again and again? I can't understand her previous partners. Why did they make her feel like she takes too long to come, when she barely took any time at all?

And the way she watched herself in the mirror...

I think that was new for her, and I loved it. She looks like a goddess; of *course* she should enjoy watching herself.

I wish I had a video of Yvonne riding my hand or my cock. I'd play it over and over—and I suspect she'd be turned by that, by the thought of me beating off to it.

Fuck.

I don't want to bring up making a sex tape, though. She might enjoy making one, but men have done some foul shit with such videos, and I can't expect her to trust me.

But I have lots of material for my imagination to work with. I could have spent all day fantasizing about her, but I didn't. I forced myself to do laundry, to vacuum the apartment, to eat a proper dinner.

Now that I'm in the shower, I don't restrain myself. I recall her wet, welcoming heat. Her hands plucking her nipples. The way she was so uninhibited around me, the way she was mesmerized by the sight of me pounding her from behind.

It doesn't take long.

I haven't gotten her out of my system, but that's okay; I didn't expect once to be enough.

Sunday morning, after a better sleep than I've had in weeks, I get a text from Evan. He says he bought a couple of mooncakes for me. We both like red bean mooncakes with multiple egg yolks—I like the salted egg because it cuts down on the sweetness—while the other members of our family prefer the lotus ones.

Hearing from one of my brothers...it cuts through some of the haze I've been in since yesterday afternoon. Brings me back down to Earth. Reminds me of how damn complicated this situation is.

I can have Yvonne, but only in private. Nobody can know.

For starters, I'm sure some people would find the timing suspicious. They'd assume she was cheating on Carl with me—and that's why she ran.

But I'd never sleep with someone who was engaged. (Well, maybe if they were in an open relationship, but that's not something that's happened to me.) After all, I know how it feels to have my girlfriend cheat.

Still, sleeping with Carl's ex is probably against some kind of code, even if he's my cousin, not my brother. Though we're not close, it seems wrong.

I wouldn't say I have regrets now, not exactly...

Yet I feel way more uneasy than I did yesterday, even if there's no reason that anyone would discover what Yvonne and I did.

I need to get out.

I tell Evan that I'll pick up the mooncakes since I'm heading out soon anyway—a drive up north will do me good. Maybe I'll go to Lake Simcoe.

Escape the city, and escape the prickle of unease that has settled inside me.

Chapter 20

Yvonne

Monday evening, I'm tending to my plants when I get a call. It's Shauna, so I answer.

"Hey!" she says. "I found you an apartment."

"You did?"

"Yes! My cousin—well, she's not technically my cousin, but you know what I mean—and her husband are looking for a tenant. I said you could go see it tomorrow after work—I hope that's okay? Then if you want it, it's yours."

Shauna gives me the details about the unit. It's smaller and not as close to transit as I'd like, but it's as much as I can hope for within my budget. And the idea of actually having a place of my own, of not having this hanging over my head, is enough to make me excited.

"I'll be there tomorrow," I say. "Thank you so much, Shauna. I really appreciate it."

"No problem."

"I have some news, too." I pause. "I slept with Leo."

"I thought he said no?"

"He changed his mind."

"Oh my God!" she shrieks. "Was it good?"

"Yeah, it was amazing." I can't help smiling.

"Tell me everything."

"I'm not telling you *everything*."

"Boo."

"But he has this rule," I say. "We can't do it in the bed—like, at all—"

"*What?*"

"Why are you being so loud? You're going to destroy my hearing."

"Fine. I'll talk at a so-called normal volume—"

I laugh.

"—just tell me why he has this rule."

"I'm not sure, but I had to agree to it before he took me to his apartment. I guess he doesn't want me to forget that it's only sex."

"And you wanted that dick so badly—"

"Shauna!" I hiss. "I'm at his parents' house."

"Are they listening to this conversation?

"No, but still."

"Where did you do it?" she asks.

"Uh, on a chair."

"Yvonne!"

"I thought you weren't going to destroy my hearing anymore? And it's not that shocking. A chair is hardly a weird place to have sex. It's not, like, on a horse."

"A *horse*?" she whisper-yells.

"I swear I read it in a book once."

"Which book? I'm writing it down."

I chuckle. "Look, my life isn't that dramatic.

"Well, I'm just happy it was amazing. I assume that means he was better than Carl?"

"Yeah, definitely."

"Was he bigger? Do you have a ruler handy? Pull it out and estimate for me."

Neither of us says anything for several seconds because we're too busy laughing.

It's nice to have a friend who's known me for a long time. I bet Shauna's thinking of a conversation we had years ago, back when we were inexperienced teenagers. We were reading about dick sizes and pulled out a ruler. *Eight inches? Sounds painful*, I remember saying.

Leo is actually smaller than my ex-fiancé. I'd feel weird saying that out loud, but it's true. Leo is about average-sized, based on my limited experience, and Carl was definitely aware that he was bigger than average. Maybe that's part of the reason he didn't feel the need to try very hard in bed, I don't know. Sometimes it was a little painful, and he'd get annoyed when I asked for extra lube.

Shauna doesn't push me to answer her size question. "When are you going to see him next?"

"We didn't discuss it, though we agreed we'd do it again. You can't tell anyone, okay?"

"I promise." She pauses. "I've been meaning to ask about your honeymoon. Did you cancel it?"

"Oh, crap."

In the mess of looking for an apartment, I'd forgotten about that. Luckily, the accommodation can be canceled with a week's notice—less a small deposit—so I still have time.

But I kinda want to go. I have the days off work.

"You want to come with me?" I ask. "Just the two of us. It'll be fun. You can pick the music in the car."

"Well, we'd be taking my car," she says, "since you don't have one, so that only seems fair. What are the dates again?"

I tell her, then wait while she looks at her calendar.

"Sorry," she says. "My coworker will be on vacation then. I know I won't be able to get the time off."

My mood drops.

Maybe I could rent a car. That's an expense I don't need right now, though, especially with the amount it'll cost to buy furniture and move.

"But back to Leo," she says. "You should text him."

"As soon as I get off the phone with you."

We talk for another half hour.

ME: Hey! You free on Thursday? I could come over.

A minute later, I still don't have a response from Leo, and I start to freak out. He agreed that we should do it again, but what if he changed his mind? What if he has some other woman he fucks every Thursday night? What if...

LEO: Sorry, I was in the shower. Thursday evening is good for me.

I exhale slowly. I got worked up over nothing.

LEO: Come over to do what?

Does he want me to text dirty things to him? Or does he just want to be absolutely clear? It would help if he'd added a winky face.

A moment later, I do receive an emoji, but it's not that one.

No, it's an eggplant.

I bark out a laugh and hope it didn't disrupt the other people in the house—his parents!—since it's a bit late. I get cozy under the covers.

ME: Yes, I'd like to eat some eggplant parmesan with you. Sounds delicious.

ME: I've been thinking about being with you again...a lot.

It's not as scary to text those words as it would be to say them out loud, and when I get his response, there's a flutter in my chest.

LEO: Me too

On Thursday, I tell Leo my exciting news as soon as he opens the door.

"I found an apartment!" I say, and he pulls me against him.

"We should celebrate," he murmurs into my neck.

And we do.

He devours my mouth, and his hands roam my body until I'm a puddle of need. Then he fucks me against the wall and over the arm of his couch.

Afterward, we sit on the couch, and I drape my legs over his and tell him more about my apartment. We stay there for half an hour, and I suspect this isn't how booty calls usually end.

For a moment, I wonder if we could have something more, but I quickly dismiss the possibility. No, I'm just making the most of my single life.

"Do you have plans tomorrow evening?" I ask.

Chapter 21

Leo

On Friday, Yvonne comes to my door in a trench coat. She opens it up to reveal a clingy, lowcut shirt that I suspect she never wore in her old life.

Yet she's wearing it now. For me.

There's a split second of uncertainty on her face, but then I say "beautiful," the word nearly sticking in my throat, and kiss her.

I still can't believe I get to do that. Any feelings of uneasiness go out the window when I see her. There's no space for them.

I have plans for Yvonne.

I turn us around so that she's facing the mirror, and I stand behind her and kiss the side of her neck. "You like watching yourself."

"Yes." Her cheeks pinken. She's a bit embarrassed, but she didn't deny it.

"You should. Because you look amazing." I roll my hips against her, my erection rubbing her ass. "This is what you do to me. Even when you're not here. I think of you, and..."

Her eyes flutter closed.

"No," I say. "Keep watching. Look at how much you want it."

I'm speaking more than the last two times. It doesn't come naturally to me, but I know I'll have to talk her through this...if she's interested in my plan.

"I thought I could take pictures or videos of you."

She stiffens against me.

When I first thought of filming us, I immediately discarded the idea. But it wouldn't leave my mind, and I tried to think of what might make her feel safe enough to do it.

"I have an old phone," I say. "We can use that, and you can keep it. I won't have any copies myself. You'll have full control over it, and I'll never ask for it back."

I'd love to have a copy, of course, but I can't expect her to trust me like that.

"Ohhh," she says slowly.

I'm still standing behind her, but I don't kiss her. I don't run my hands over her body. As I wait for her answer, I feel uncomfortably exposed. Maybe in those sentences I spoke, she senses my exact desire for her, desire that started the day I met her, desire that goes beyond wanting to bury my cock inside her.

I want to show her...herself. I want her to discover that with me.

"Okay." She nods. "Okay."

I take a moment to steady myself. Then I gesture toward the couch, where I've laid out a towel, and hold up my old phone. She sits down, legs stretch out on the couch, and leans against the arm.

"Lovely," I say. "Now show me your tits."

There's a split second of hesitation before she pulls her shirt over her head. Hands on the clasp of her bra, she says, "You have to do it, too."

I set down the phone, tear off my shirt, and appreciate the hungry way she drinks me in. She holds my gaze as she removes her bra.

"Touch them for me," I say.

She cups her breasts and brushes one thumb over her nipple. I take a few pictures. The lighting isn't great, but as always, Yvonne seems to capture the light there is and make the most of it.

"Take off your pants."

I remove mine first, and then she unzips her jeans and shimmies out of them. They land on the floor. There's a hint of shyness in her expression.

"Do you want to stop?" I ask.

She shakes her head.

I hiss out a breath. "Your underwear."

I keep mine on, but she removes hers, leaving them on top of her discarded jeans. I grab one of the chairs—in fact, I happen to know it's *the* chair—and pull it closer to the couch. I sit down.

"Spread your legs," I say, "and I'll take a picture."

She hesitates, but she still doesn't ask to stop.

I slip my cock through the hole in my boxers and leisurely stroke it with the hand that's not holding the phone.

She watches avidly. "Film yourself."

That's now how I expected this to go, but I press record and stroke myself a few times. The act of filming myself doesn't do anything for me, but the way she's watching me...that does.

"Your turn," I say.

She opens her legs, presenting her pussy to me, and she looks like a queen. I almost pinch myself to make sure that this isn't my imagination, that Yvonne really is in my apartment, posing for me on my couch.

I wet my lips and zoom in on her crotch.

Fuck, I'm desperate to bury my face between her thighs, but I restrain myself. For now. Her hair is neatly trimmed, and she looks utterly delectable.

"Now touch yourself," I say.

She hesitates once again. "I want you to film yourself...touching me. When I watch..." She trails off and covers her mouth.

"When you watch porn, Yvonne?"

"I don't do it very often."

"Mm."

"I really don't, but when I do, I like seeing women...getting fingered."

I pull the chair up to the couch. My cock is painfully hard, but I don't touch it. Instead, I start recording, and then I slip my middle finger inside her.

"Oh," she says. "*Ohhh.*"

I think she's playing it up for the camera, and I'm certainly not complaining.

"Good—" I snap my mouth shut, realizing that probably isn't what she wants to hear. Yvonne is used to being the good girl, but with me...

"You're such a bad girl."

She clenches around me.

Yeah, I think I was right.

"Naked in a strange man's apartment," I say. "Letting him touch you."

I remove my finger, and she bucks toward my hand, whimpering at the loss...but then I slap her pussy, and she gasps.

"So very, very wet for me," I murmur as I slip my finger back inside.

I zoom out so I can capture her face. The desperation. The pleasure. She's fucking incredible, and the fact that she likes when I do this to her...I'll become a cocky bastard if I don't watch out.

I zoom in on her expression, and I can see the moment I add a second finger. I'm sure the video is utter shit—my hand is shaking—but I continue to hold up the phone.

"What about sucking me off?" I ask. "Should I film that?"

She squeezes her thighs together. "Yes."

Fuck me.

I climb onto the couch, get up on my knees, and hold my cock to her lips. I film her taking me inside her mouth...and then she looks up at me, looks up at the camera.

Yeah, I can't do this anymore. I need both of my hands.

I stop recording, fling the phone onto the coffee table, and grab a condom.

"Leo," she whispers as she positions herself on her back. She looks at me like she needs me more than anything.

I slam into her, and she cries out.

"Leo, I'm almost..."

I lick my finger and drop it between us. I find her clit, and two strokes later, she's coming apart on my cock.

I hold myself steady for a few moments and gaze down at her, beautifully disheveled on my couch. It's not going to take long for me, either.

But first, I have to kiss her. Somehow, I haven't kissed her at all today, and that must be fixed. I lean down and press my lips to hers. She immediately responds, kissing me back as she wraps her legs around my lower back, and I groan. Her mouth is exactly what I needed, and now, I feel complete.

Our lips fused together, I slowly begin moving again, and her tongue is on mine, her breasts against my chest, when I find my release inside her.

I continue to kiss her as I pull out, unable to let go.

.♥.♥.♥.♥.♥.

When she returns from the washroom, I hand her the phone. "Put it in your purse so you don't forget."

She does, then she climbs back on the couch and snuggles up against me...and drops a bombshell.

"Carl cheated on me."

"He *what*?"

What the hell is wrong with my cousin? If she were mine, there is no fucking way I'd do something so horrible. I wouldn't be tempted.

Seriously, what the fuck?

"Back in May," she says. "Well, I don't know when it started, but that's when I found out." She shuts her eyes. "I should have ended it then, but I didn't."

Yvonne doesn't need my righteous fury right now, so I try to push that aside.

"Why not?" I ask gently.

"The sunk cost fallacy." She chuckles.

I have no idea what that is, but I can look it up later.

"I know it sounds like I have no self-respect," she says, no mirth in her voice now. "But it was too overwhelming to imagine blowing up my life. I'd been planning the wedding for almost two years, it was so close... And we were perfect for each other. Well, I was perfect for him—it sounds conceited to say that, but I'd make just the right kind of wife. I have a decent, respectable job, but nothing approaching his earning potential, so I could stay at home with the kids for a few years. I'm good at organizing things and getting things done, but I'd never outshine him."

That's a bunch of bullshit. She'd outshine anyone.

"If a friend had come to me with this dilemma," she continues, "I would have told her to dump him, but I did ask a friend—my maid of honor—and she said I should go through with the wedding." She sighs. "We're not speaking anymore."

"Good."

"I felt like I was lacking, like something was wrong with me."

"No," I say, pulling her on top of me. "Absolutely not. This was about him, not you. But I get it. My high school girlfriend...she slept with my best friend. I caught them together."

"Leo—"

"It's fine. It was a long time ago now. I'm over it."

But back then, it was another example of how I wasn't enough for anyone. I wasn't very smart, I wasn't a good student...

This is actually the first time I've told someone that I caught them in the act. My family just knows that she moved on from me to my so-called best friend, and I let them to draw their own conclusions.

"Even if you don't..." I pinch my brow. "Even if you *know* it doesn't make sense, sometimes it still *feels* like the truth."

"Yes, exactly." She smiles at me. "But you've made me feel sexy, in a way I've never felt before. Thank you."

"Again, you don't have to thank me for sex." I pause. "You ended my dry spell. I hadn't slept with anyone in years."

"Years?"

"Since before the pandemic. Just sorta happened."

"You were wasting your talents."

I chuckle, trying not to feel too pleased at her words, and run a hand through her hair as she settles against me. It seems like a luxury to curl up with her like this.

We're quiet for a few minutes, and just when I think she might have fallen asleep, she lifts her head and says, "Do you have any vacation days left?"

"Yeah, I have a week."

"Want to go on my honeymoon?"

"Your honeymoon?" I splutter.

"Carl didn't want to book a lot of time off, so it's only four nights."

God, it feels wrong to consider this, but I'm already sleeping with her, and fucking Carl doesn't deserve my guilt.

"I'll pretend I'm going with Shauna," she says, "because I wouldn't want your parents or anyone else to know."

"Finger Lakes, right?"

"Yeah. It's about a five-hour drive."

"Send me the dates." If it's just a few days, it'll probably be okay.

Logistically, that is.

It'll be a romantic trip, of sorts—and it's dangerous to think any real romance is possible. I know she's not looking for a relationship right now.

But even if I know it's a terrible idea, I can't help agreeing to spend more time with her. Agreeing to go on the honeymoon with her.

After all, I was never the smart one.

Chapter 22

Yvonne

It's late when I return to Lynne and Howie's house, but they've left the front hall light on for me. As quietly as possible, I remove my shoes, then tiptoe upstairs and get ready for bed.

In my bedroom—I've started to think of it as mine, even though it's not—I put on my pajamas and get under the covers. Then I pull the old phone out of my purse, feeling like I'm doing something illicit. When I see the first picture of myself, topless, I cover my face, embarrassed.

It's not the first time that a guy has suggested he take dirty pictures of me. Carl didn't, but another ex did, and I declined. The idea of someone having those photos on his phone... *No*.

But Leo didn't ask for the pictures for himself. He wanted them for *me*. Because he'd seen me watching myself in the mirror, and he thought I'd enjoy it.

As I flip through the pictures, I start to feel less embarrassed, despite my increasing level of nudity. I look good. The photos aren't works of art, but they're better than quick photos taken on an old phone ought to be. I wonder if it's thanks to Leo's artistic side?

In one photo, I've got a look on my face that could actually be called seductive. I've never seen myself like that before, and I stare at it for a long time.

Then I get to the videos. I watch them without the sound, of course. My ears are attuned to any noise in the rest of the house. If I hear one footstep, I'll turn off the phone and throw it in my purse and hop under the covers.

But the house is silent.

On the screen, Leo slides a finger inside me. It's a close-up of him touching me, and I can see that I'm very wet. I'm sure I'd hear it, too, if I had the volume on.

I've never watched myself being touched like this before—it's not an angle I can get in real life. It's weird but also thrilling, and I clench my thighs and remember how it felt to have his fingers inside me. The intense look he gets on his face, like he's giving my pleasure the utmost attention.

Then there's the video of me sucking him off.

A part of me is horrified that this exists, and I nearly press delete...but I can't do it. I like the evidence that I'm not the good girl I pretended to be for so long.

He called me "bad," and I loved it.

And he fucked me on the couch, and he made me come faster than I ever had before. I think that was partly thanks to the situation, the mental element, not just the way he touched me—but it never takes me too long to orgasm with him. Apparently, I just needed someone who knows what they're doing and is attentive to my needs.

I turn off the phone and put it away, and as I drift off to sleep, I think of him.

Saturday morning, Lynne lets me borrow her car again. I drive to my mother's, where there's a cloth bag bursting with containers of food for my sister, as well as a small gift wrapped in red paper.

I don't go beyond the front hall, just stand on the mat as she asks for updates on the baby.

"I got an apartment," I tell my mother before I leave. "I'm signing the papers after I visit Tracey."

"I still don't understand why you had to run. You were never the *dramatic* one."

I begin listing off my reasons. "He wants kids, and I don't. He loves the idea of a wife like me, and I...I didn't really love him. And, as I told you, he cheated on me."

"Aiyah. Life isn't one of those Disney movies."

"I know I can't expect a man to be perfect, but why should I have settled for someone who—"

"Is rich? Comes from a good family?"

"Ma, stop. I don't regret it."

She clucks her tongue. "Fine. You don't care how I feel." There's an odd vulnerability on her face that makes me want to argue with her words. I *do* care about her feelings, but not at the expense of what's best for me.

I give her a quick hug. "I'll bring everything to Tracey's right away."

"She can set the containers aside, and you will bring them back to me later."

"Yes, sometime in October."

Ma opens her mouth, but she doesn't say anything, just waves me away.

At my sister's apartment, I put the food in the fridge while she's nursing. There are piles of good stuff—Ma certainly didn't skimp. One container is entirely cut-up pineapple, which was always Tracey's favorite.

The gift in my hands, I settle on the couch beside my sister.

"His name is Isaac," she says.

"Isaac," I murmur, shaking his little foot.

"Do you not like it?"

I straighten up. "What? I didn't say that."

"No, but…" She sighs, and there's something in that sigh that sounds like Ma. Not that I mention it, of course. "You were always judging me when we were younger. That's part of the reason I never told you I was pregnant. I thought you'd say I wasn't ready, and I didn't want to hear you echo one of my greatest fears."

"I'm sorry. I wish I'd been more like you as a kid."

She just laughs.

"I'm serious," I say. "I never learned to stand up for myself and figure out what *I* want. It would have saved me a lot of issues later on."

"It's weird to hear you say that."

"I know."

We're quiet as we both look down at Isaac. I wonder what he'll be like as he grows up, how he'll challenge his parents, but I'm confident that Tracey will let him be his own person, rather than using him to live out her dreams. When I told her that she'd be a good mom, I wasn't lying. I believe it.

Once Isaac has finished nursing, she hands him to me and starts opening the gift.

"This is from your po po," she says, putting his little hand on the paper when she's partway through.

It's a onesie. Tracey unfolds it, and something falls to the floor. A red envelope with a bunch of fifty-dollar bills.

"She didn't need to do this," my sister says.

I don't tell her that I'm not willing to be the go-between forever, nor do I tell her that she should allow Mom to visit. I trust her to make her own choices.

When Tracey's in the shower, I whisper to Isaac, "I'm not going to give you any cousins, but I'll be the best auntie, I promise."

He replies with a fart.

I go to Leo's apartment two more times in the next week. After we have sex, I always stay for a little while. We snuggle on the couch, which doesn't seem all that different from snuggling on a bed, but I don't try to push his boundary.

However...

"I tried to change the room at the bed and breakfast," I say. "To one with two beds, I mean. But there was nothing available. I have one more day to cancel it and try to find something else, but—"

"No, it's fine. Just for the trip."

"Are you sure? You don't need to say things are fine when they're not." I've become aware of just how much I used to do that.

"Really, it's okay," he says softly, running his hand through my hair.

I don't know why he's okay with it now, but I let it go. I'm excited to share a bed with him, truth be told.

One evening, a few days before the trip, I write out the instructions for my plants and show Lynne what to do while I'm gone. I make little name tags with toothpicks, which I put in the pots so she knows who is who.

"I'm glad Shauna is able to go on your honeymoon with you," she says. "You will have a nice girls' trip, yes?"

A stab of guilt hits me. I've been lying about my companion for the trip because it would seem too weird to admit that Leo is going with me. I worry that Lynne, who's been nothing but kind to me, might lose respect for me if she had any idea what I was doing.

"You look more relaxed these days," she says.

I suspect it has something to do with all the sex, but I don't say that out loud. "It's a relief to finally have an apartment lined up."

Which is also true.

I officially get my apartment on Sunday, but I'll be in upstate New York then, so I'm not moving until Thursday, after the trip.

"You should take this." Lynne points to the bookshelf in the room, then the dresser.

"I can't—"

"Ah, why do we need all these things? I know you want your own bed—you prefer a queen, not a twin, yes?—but we have too much. I insist."

One of the exciting parts about finally having my own apartment? I can organize and decorate it however I like. When Shauna and I were in our last year of high school, we used to go to IKEA and dream about having a place that was entirely our own.

However, I need to be smart with my money, and even if some things here aren't exactly what I'd pick myself, they're solid. Still...

"How would we move them?" I ask. "Easier to get one big shipment from IKEA."

"Aiyah! You're so difficult! Aaron has a truck. We'll borrow it."

Aaron is one of Carl and Leo's cousins. I vaguely remember him.

"If you're sure—" I begin.

"I said I insisted."

That stab of guilt hits me again, but I push it aside, as I've pushed aside so many other feelings in the past.

Yet it returns a few hours later. I'm going on my honeymoon with another man, and I'm lying to nearly everyone about it. Howie is driving me to Shauna's that morning, and Leo is picking me up there.

It seems wrong.

Friday morning, I'm on the bus when I receive an email from Mary.

When I was a summer student at the same place where I work now, Mary was my boss. An older white lady nearing retirement, she acted as a mentor of sorts.

One day, she came to my desk and asked for an update on the project I was working on. I hated the surprise, but I thought I pulled it off.

Then she asked me to come to her office, and she shut the door.

I knew I was getting in trouble—unusual for me—but I didn't understand why. I took a seat across from her fancy office chair. She didn't sit down; she stayed standing and crossed her arms.

"Don't do that," she said.

"D-do what?" I stammered.

"Tell me what you think I want to hear."

"That's not what I'm doing?" It came out as a question...because it was a lie.

I was doing it because I thought that was how you kept a job. It was also how I wrote papers in school, and it had served me well.

She sighed. "I know it's different for women than it is for men. A woman offers a few small opinions in a meeting and is told she's dominating the conversation. I've been labeled a troublemaker for doing very little." She shook her head. "But I genuinely want to know what you think—and why, of course. Otherwise, what's the purpose of having you do the work? So tomorrow, we'll do this again, and you won't try to contort the data to tell me what would be easiest. Understood?"

Trembling, I nodded.

And that was why, when I was offered a full-time job there after graduation, I took it.

Sure, I still had to play office politics a little, but Mary had meant her words, though it took me a while to fully trust her. She retired a year ago, and while I don't like my new boss quite as much, I'm still happy with my job.

Could I make more money elsewhere? Maybe, but having a job I don't mind is worth something, and people actually care about what I think there. I didn't fully grasp the importance of that before. Sure, it was uncomfortable when my coworkers discovered I didn't actually get married, but I've been dealing with the fall-out in every part of my life, and while there were some whispers a month ago, a colleague's divorce is occupying the gossips now.

Someone must have told Mary that I didn't get married. I invited her to the wedding, but she was on an extended six-month trip with her wife. She'd offered to check on my plants when I went on my honeymoon, though.

I'm in the middle of typing a response—to suggest we catch up over coffee in a few weeks—when I get a series of texts from my cousin Erin's phone. Given the bizarre collection of letters and numbers, followed by a picture of the floor, I doubt they're from Erin herself; I suspect her youngest kid got a hold of her phone.

By the time I arrive at the office, I have an apology from my cousin for the thirteen messages before eight in the morning, as well as a question about how I'm doing. Overwhelmed at the thought of answering with any degree of honesty, I simply tell her that I'm fine and will be going on my honeymoon with a friend.

Then I open up Excel and admire my spreadsheets, which aren't near as messy as my life.

"Francine," I whisper late that evening, when the rest of the house is shrouded in darkness, "I'm not making a mistake, am I? It's just a trip with a friend, right? A fun trip that will involve lots of sex. An extended booty call in another country. Perfectly normal."

She doesn't reply. She's probably confused by the concept of booty calls.

"Do you think it means anything that you're a snake plant and he has a snake tattoo?"

Francine, sensibly, remains quiet, perhaps reflecting on the fact that snake plants have many other names, including Saint George's sword and mother-in-law's tongue. Heh.

I say goodnight to the rest of my plants and turn out the light.

Yvonne's Search History

- Finger Lakes wineries and breweries

- Finger Lakes waterfalls

- Taughannock Falls trails

- Ithaca hidden gems

- Ithaca weather forecast

- am I an exhibitionist

Chapter 23

Leo

I can't believe I'm on a trip with Yvonne. But there she is, dozing off in the seat beside me as I approach the border.

I tap her shoulder. "Hey."

"What...oh." She yawns and takes her passport out of her purse.

The customs officer—or whatever his job title is—looks at our passports and asks why we're going to the US.

"Vacation," I say.

I've crossed the border by car a number of times. I've never had a problem, but it still makes me nervous. And he's probably making assumptions that aren't correct; Yvonne and I aren't in a relationship, but I'm not going to explain anything unless asked.

Fortunately, it's not long before he waves us through.

From the border, it's over an hour to Letchworth State Park, our first stop. Apparently, the park is called the "Grand Canyon of the East," which makes it sound important, but I hadn't heard of it before Yvonne mentioned it earlier this week. I barely had to do any planning for this trip. She just asked a few questions about what I like to do when I travel, and she assured me she had it all figured out.

As we near Letchworth, I can't help thinking about how she'd planned to do this with another man. Driving with a napping companion gives me lots of time alone in my thoughts, which isn't a great place to be.

Eventually, I park the car, and a short walk takes us to the first powerful falls in the canyon. It's a beautiful late September day. The sky is blue, with the occasional fluffy white cloud, and the leaves on the trees are mostly green, but some are turning yellow and orange.

And being outside of my usual life...it makes my angst retreat.

I take pictures of Yvonne with her phone, but it feels like we have an unspoken agreement not to take any of *us*. Because if anyone saw them, it would be suspicious.

After we're finished viewing all the falls, Yvonne directs me to a brewery for a late lunch. We sit on the patio and eat burgers, and it reminds me of the first time we ate together, the day she didn't get married. Over a month ago now.

But remembering that doesn't cause me discomfort, and I'm able to relax and enjoy a nice meal outside with a gorgeous woman, even if there's no vinegar for our fries. I've got five days with her, and I'm going to make the most of it.

A few strands of hair have escaped Yvonne's ponytail, and they fly up in the breeze; I itch to reach out and tuck them behind her ear. Since we're not in Toronto, there's an even lower chance than usual of an acquaintance seeing us.

So I do it, and she doesn't pull back.

We continue driving, stopping a couple of times to view smaller falls, and reach the bed and breakfast around five o'clock. Yvonne is chatty with the woman who shows us to our room. I don't have to do anything other than carry our bags.

When we step inside the room and close the door behind us, my attention is focused on the bed. It's an actual canopy bed—I've never slept in one of those before. Though even if it were just an ordinary bed, it would be exciting because I'd get to share it with *her*.

The room, which is larger than my entire apartment, is all heavy wood furniture, nothing cheap, and the walls are cream. A door at the far end takes us to a private second-floor balcony. We're surrounded by trees, so it's nice and quiet. On another wall, there's a bay window with what looks like a reading nook. The washroom has a jacuzzi.

It's beautiful and excessive—but tasteful—and I briefly feel like I don't belong. Like I'm an interloper on this vacation.

Which I sort of am.

But then Yvonne opens her suitcase and starts undressing in front of me, and I forget about that. I wrap my arms around her as I kiss the side of her neck.

"Leo!" she says. "I need to have a shower and get ready for dinner. We have reservations."

I don't see why she needs to change. She looks perfect as she is. I slide us toward the full-length mirror so she can see herself. I know the mirror will remind her of other things.

However, she has more self-control than I do, and she pushes me back with a laugh. "Seriously, we only have an hour."

"Plenty of time."

"Later," she says, then makes a show of shedding the rest of her clothes on the way to the washroom.

Fuck me.

Since it'll take me all of ten minutes to get ready, I waste time on my phone before putting on some gray pants and ironing a black dress shirt. I know she'll look better than me, but I don't want to be a complete slob—she deserves more than that.

When she emerges, she's wearing a little black dress, strappy heels, and some kind of ribbon necklace. She's breathtaking.

"What do you think?" She twirls around.

I don't say anything. My jaw doesn't seem to be working properly.

Finally, I manage to get it unhinged, but the sound that comes out of my mouth sounds more like a growl that anything else.

She frowns.

Shit. Does she think I'm unhappy with how she looks, rather than stunned speechless?

I walk over to her, rolling up my sleeves along the way, as though I'm about to get down to business—the business of getting her naked and sullying her up.

Except I won't do that now because I know she wouldn't want it.

Not yet.

"You're..." Okay, I've found my voice, but I seem to have forgotten all words in the English language—or any other language. "Beautiful."

It seems horribly insufficient, but it's all I can manage.

"Really," I add, because I'm just so great at communicating.

I cup the back of her head, careful not to make a mess of her hair, and press a slow kiss to her forehead. She sighs in contentment, and that sigh is nearly enough to make me tear off her clothing, but instead, we go to dinner.

The steak and seafood restaurant where Yvonne has made reservations is about a ten-minute drive away, on one of the finger-shaped lakes. It's dusk when we arrive, and we're shown to a table by a window overlooking the dark water. The table is lit by a single candle.

I try not to grimace when I open the menu. The prices aren't cheap, made worse by the fact that they're in American dollars.

But it's just one meal. I can manage.

I don't get anything to drink. Yvonne orders a glass of wine, and we start with a small order of oysters. They've never really been my thing, but watching her eat them is a different matter.

That's definitely my thing.

We split the tomato salad, scattered with fresh herbs, before our mains arrive: crab for her, and the smallest and cheapest steak on the menu for me.

"I want to take your parents out for dinner," she says, "to thank them for letting me stay at their house. They also insisted on helping me move."

Her mention of my parents breaks some of the romantic haze of the night, but somehow, in the dim light of the restaurant, the candlelight flickering in her eyes...it's easy to get caught up in the moment again.

"My dad likes the Keg," I say. "He thinks it's the greatest thing ever."

"And your mom?"

"There's a Cantonese-style lobster place...I forget the name, but I know where it is. I'll send you a link."

"Thanks. I'll make sure they don't try to pay."

"Good luck."

"I might need it. I don't want to resort to stuffing bills in their wallets."

I like that she always tries to show her appreciation for people. Carl, on the other hand, probably took her for granted. So, although it doesn't come naturally to me, I say, "Thank you for, uh. Inviting me on this trip. Planning everything."

She smiles at me. "I like planning vacations. The wedding—now that was a different matter. But travel research is fun."

She leans forward, and there's something about the shadows on her collarbone...I've never been so captivated by a woman's collarbone before.

Under the table, I place my hand on her knee.

"I did make a few changes to my initial itinerary," she says. "Back in May, I'd planned a hot-air balloon ride at Letchworth Park, but..."

Yeah, Carl might be able to afford shit like that, but I can't. Though I never cared about being rich, now I wish I had more money so I could spend it on her.

For dessert, she orders a chocolate torte with raspberry something-or-other, and I have a taste. When she goes to the washroom afterward, I ask for the bill and pay. I'm just sliding my credit card back into my wallet when she returns.

"Leo." She gives me a look. "You shouldn't have."

She doesn't say anything else; she just links her arm through mine and leads me to the front of the restaurant. Like we really are on a real date. Like she really is mine and she's happy to be seen with me.

I hold myself back from kissing her.

We wind our way to the bed and breakfast on dark, quiet roads. As soon as we're in the room, I set my lips to hers, pausing only to pull her dress over her head.

She looks questioningly at the mattress.

I pick her up, walk over to the bed, and lay her down on her back. As I hold myself above her, I admire the way her hair fans out over the pillows. There's something luxurious about actually being in a bed together. It makes me feel like I have all the time in the world.

I remove her bra and lavish attention on her breasts, first with my hands, then with my mouth. She releases breathy little sighs that go straight to my cock, which strains against the zipper of my pants. I tug down her underwear and toss them aside. I kiss my way from the inside of her knee to the top of her thigh…and then I do the same to the other side.

She moans and bucks against my face; I like that she isn't shy about what she wants from me. I lick around her entrance, dipping my tongue inside before circling her clit, and she grips the back of my head.

"Leo."

It's the only thing she's said in a long time, and I'm not complaining. When I took pictures of her and filmed her—that time, I was talking a lot, but today, we're both quiet.

I slip my fingers inside her and curl them in the way she likes, and one of her hands clenches the blanket. She tastes amazing. I wish I could do this every single day of my life, and as she smiles at me with hooded eyes, I think…maybe that's possible.

Tonight, anything seems possible.

I can feel her tensing, getting closer, and then she shudders against my face. I crawl up her body, fully clothed against her skin; she immediately begins unbuttoning my shirt, her fingers clumsier than usual. She pushes the edges of my shirt aside and slides her hands up my chest, kissing me as she brushes her fingertips over my nipple.

When she shoves me back between her legs, I smile against her pussy, glad she's being greedy. She's different than she was the first time we were together. I love seeing her splayed out in bed, taking what she wants. Opening up to me.

I lift my head and remove my fingers from her body. She moans in protest, then holds my gaze as I paint her thighs with her moisture, my hand moving in lazy swirls. When I shove my fingers back inside, she gasps.

I want to become an expert in all her sounds.

Unable to stand it any longer, I remove my pants and boxers. My hands shake as I roll on the condom, and I rub myself over her entrance without pushing inside. She squirms, and I don't make her wait any longer; I thrust all the way in.

She muffles her cry against my chest.

I fuck her with long, languid strokes, just because I can. Just because she's not bent over a chair and she doesn't have to go back to my parents' house anytime soon. I roll my hips against hers like I have all the time in the world, and I kiss her slowly, reverently.

She tilts her body to the right, and I let her flip us over so she's riding me. Seated on top of me like a queen, bathed in the light behind her.

She adjusts her position—to get the perfect friction on her clit, I think—then speeds up her pace. I grip her hips and pump into her again and again, until we come together, and afterward, she flops next to me on the mattress and laughs like she hasn't a care in the world.

After showering, I climb back into bed in a T-shirt and boxers. Yvonne is wearing pink pajamas, and it seems very intimate to see her dressed for bed, to spend the night with her.

She strokes the skin between my eyebrows, as if trying to smooth it.

"Hey," she murmurs. "What's wrong?"

"Nothing," I say immediately.

Except I'm starting to think I can keep you, but I know I can't.

It's one thing for us to screw around without telling anyone, but if we were to have a relationship, I wouldn't want it to be secret. Not for long, anyway.

Yet how could I tell people that I'm seeing the woman who left my cousin at the altar?

I don't feel that bad for Carl—the fucker cheated on her, after all—but what would our families think? My mother only just told me that she thinks I've done well in life, and this would destroy her view of me.

Besides, I'm not in the same league as Yvonne. I knew that from the moment I met her. She's just having fun with me. Enjoying her freedom.

I know it's temporary, I know it isn't real life, but God, this is the reason I had those rules for myself. And now we're not just sharing a bed; we're on a damn romantic getaway.

If I'm honest, I was already in deep trouble before today. Although I had a thing for Yvonne from the beginning, the past six weeks have made it way, way worse, and it was ridiculous to think I had a hope of avoiding that with some flimsy rules.

"What did I do?" she asks.

Fuck. I don't want her to think she did a single thing wrong.

I shake my head. "Tired from driving."

Which is true. I'm a little tired, but if she slipped her hand into my boxers again, I could be ready to go in seconds.

She seems to accept this, and she curls up against me like it's the most natural thing in the world.

I'm so fucked.

Chapter 24

Yvonne

WHEN I WAKE UP on Sunday morning, the first thing I see is black ink curled around a bicep, and it takes me a few seconds to orient myself.

I'm on vacation. With Leo Mok.

He's lying on his stomach, arms crossed above his head, and it's a beautiful sight. I've never seen him asleep before. I can't help staring.

A few minutes later, he rolls over and scrubs a hand over his face. A notch appears between his eyebrows, but then his lips turn up. "Hey."

"Good morning," I say.

It's very quiet in the room. There are none of the city sounds that I'm used to. Just a few birds chirping.

I smile, unable to contain myself. We've got four days together, and by the look of the early sun filtering through the curtains, it's going to be a beautiful day, like the forecast promised. I can't wait to get started.

I slide toward the edge of the bed, but a strong arm pulls me back. My chest is flush with Leo's, and his morning wood is unmistakable.

He kisses my neck and murmurs something. I can barely make out the words, but I think he says, "I can't believe you're actually here with me."

His lips slide lower. As he approaches my breasts, I feel a frisson of excitement, except...

"We don't have time for this."

"Hmm?" he says from the vicinity of my covered nipple. He pulls it into his mouth, and I groan before pushing him back.

"We have a lot to do today, and it's already eight. Breakfast ends at nine."

He rolls his tongue over the tight bud, and I instinctively arch against him before he leans back. He gives me a wink, accompanied by a crooked smile.

Oh my God. When he's playful, it's irresistible.

But I have to resist. Because, like I said, we have lots to do and we need to eat.

In the washroom, I observe the wet fabric of my pajamas over my breast. I release a shuddering breath.

Later.

For breakfast, we have cheese soufflés, served with bacon and fruit salad and lots of coffee, and once we're in the car, I direct Leo toward Watkins Glen. He appears content to do whatever I have planned. The other day, I asked him what sort of things he'd like to do on the trip. He didn't say much, but he seemed keenest on the outdoor stuff.

"It's supposed to be really beautiful," I say as he pulls into the state park.

But even knowing that, I'm somehow unprepared for how beautiful it is along the gorge with all the waterfalls. We walk behind a waterfall at one point, and the sun is shining just right to produce a rainbow. I take a bunch of pictures, but none of them quite do it justice.

We grab a quick lunch—nothing big because I'm still full from breakfast—then visit a winery on the picturesque shores of a lake. There are more clouds in the sky now, but they add character to the landscape. I buy a few bottles of wine before we drive to Taughannock Falls.

Leo remains a steady presence next to me. I keep checking in with him, making sure he's okay following my plans; he always says he is.

I try not to think about how this trip would have been different with my ex. Carl would have definitely had more opinions—and there's nothing wrong with that. But as someone who's used to acquiescing to others' desires, doing what *I* want is a nice change.

After the falls, we drive into Ithaca. As we stroll through the streets and pop into the occasional store, I find myself standing closer to Leo, even reaching for his hand before I realize what I'm doing and pull back.

Holding hands is something you do in a relationship.

I push aside my unease as I enter a tapas restaurant, where we sit at a high-top table and order olives and bread and jamón and mussels escabeche. Every bite is a concentrated explosion of taste.

Leo's sleeves are rolled up, and I spend too much time admiring his forearms. I watch his fingers as he reaches for an olive, the movement of his throat as he swallows a bit of bread.

When we return to our room at the bed and breakfast, he presses me against the door and rolls his hips against me, nice and slow. His lips consume mine...and he finally finishes what he started first thing in the morning.

On Monday, I wake up to thunder. This isn't a surprise, but I'd hoped the forecast would be wrong. Alas.

Once again, Leo is lying on his stomach. I start tracing the snake tattoo with my fingertip before I realize what I'm doing.

He grunts and opens his eyes.

"Sorry, I didn't mean to wake you," I say.

I just can't help touching you.

He pulls me close, and my body molds against his. I curse the fact that breakfast ends at nine. I'd be content to stay in bed for a long time.

After we eat blueberry pancakes and sausages, we return to our room. I strip my shirt over my head, and as I drop it to the floor, there's another crack of thunder. The rain picks up, but we're safe in here. The room feels like our private sanctuary.

Leo's dark eyes gleam as he pounces, pushing me back onto the bed. As soon as I feel his weight on top of me, his cock pressing against my thigh, I can think of nothing but getting him inside me. I twist against his weight. With him, I'm a needy, sexual creature, and I love how he makes me feel. That intense gaze, focused just on *me*.

He removes the rest of my clothes and lays me, spread eagle, on the bed. He can see every inch of my body, and I don't want to hide.

No, with him I want to show off.

"You know what I'd like to do?" He rolls off the bed and rummages through his suitcase. When he returns, there's a sketchbook and a pencil in his hand. "You can say no. Or if you prefer not to be naked..."

I swallow. I've never thought about someone drawing me like this, not even when I watched *Titanic* a few years ago, though I did enjoy that scene.

But now, I want it.

"Yes," I whisper. "I'm saying *yes*."

He unties the curtains along one side of the canopy bed, letting them hang behind me. His brow furrowed in concentration, he positions me so I'm reclined on a pillow.

"Okay?" he says.

I nod. Then I instinctively smile—because that's what I do when someone snaps a picture of me—but this will take more than a few seconds, so I wipe the smile off my face and settle in.

Seated on the other side of the bed, he picks up his pencil, but he doesn't set it to the paper. Instead, he runs it over the slope of my shoulder and down my arm. My attention is focused on that single point of contact, leaving a trail of heat in its wake, and my skin prickles with awareness. When he brushes the pencil over the tip of my nipple, I shudder and wish for his mouth. God, I love how he touches me.

He puts the pencil aside and moves closer. I breathe in sharply as he slides the tip of his finger into my pussy. He pleasures me with leisurely, shallow strokes.

"I thought you were going to sketch," I say.

"I will. Just getting you ready."

After a few more strokes, he withdraws, then runs his finger along the edge of the pencil and puts the lead to paper. The finger that was just inside me...now sketching me...

He tilts the sketchbook so I can't see the page, and I groan in frustration and roll my hips. The absence of his touch is painful.

"Don't move," he says.

I obey him...mostly. He can't tell if I squeeze my inner muscles, can he?

I focus on the motion of his arm. The tiniest changes in his expression. Beyond the room? I'm only conscious of the rain beating on the roof and the path around the building. The curtains are closed, though, so I can't see it.

But even if I could, I wouldn't want to look at anything but Leo.

With each minute that passes, the need in my body grows. A part of me wants to slip my hand between my legs, but I also want to see what he'll create.

His pencil leaves the paper only to slide over my arm once more; my skin pebbles, but I try to stay still.

However, once twenty minutes have passed and the ache in my pussy still hasn't eased, I can't stand it any longer. I spread my thighs infinitesimally and slide my middle finger inside.

"Yvonne…"

"What?" I say innocently.

Leo tosses the sketchbook on the floor with a growl, flips me onto my stomach, and covers my naked body with his clothed one. "You naughty girl."

I preen. I love that he can't control himself around me.

I can hear him opening his pants. He reaches for a condom, rolls it on in one smooth move, and slams into me from behind. I jolt forward and muffle my cry in the pillow.

He fucks me with furious, insistent thrusts, his body slapping against mine. He squeezes my ass before giving it a smack.

It's overwhelming. Consuming me from the inside. I clutch the blankets and meet his thrusts, urging him to go faster, to find his release.

He stiffens and comes inside me, and not ten seconds later, he turns me onto my back, spreads my legs wide, and buries his face between my thighs. He hasn't shaved today, and his scruff abrades my skin. He slides two fingers inside me and continues to lick me until I'm shamelessly bucking against his face. Until I reach my own orgasm.

Afterward, he disposes of the condom and picks up the sketchbook.

"Can you keep still now?" he asks sternly.

"Yes," I say, but I think I might be lying.

As he finishes the drawing, I idly wonder if I'd like to do this around other people. Would I want to pose naked for anyone other than Leo? What if they watched him touch me?

I'm not sure. I've only just become acquainted with this side of myself.

But maybe, in the right circumstances...

"You can look now." He turns the picture around.

The remarkable thing is that it's clearly *me*. Even though it's not super detailed. Even though there's something extraordinarily sensual about it. Not just because I'm naked—not all nude art is sensual.

"What do you think?" he asks.

Sometimes, I can't read him. Is he nervous to show this to me? Or is he confident I'll like it? His expression gives nothing away.

My gaze snaps back to the drawing. "I love it."

He starts to rip the page out of the spiral sketchbook.

"Wait!" I set a hand on his. "What are you doing?"

"Giving it to you. You don't want it?"

"Are you sure you wouldn't like to keep it for yourself?"

"You should have it."

I think of how he insisted that I keep his old phone. He wants to make sure I control every image of me in the nude. He doesn't expect me to fully trust him, and I don't—not like I would have once trusted a man—though I'm getting close.

"Thank you," I whisper.

He smiles at me, nice and slow, and then he kisses me once more.

·♥·♥·♥·♥·♥·

It keeps raining, but I don't mind. Usually, I'd hate a rainy day on vacation, but we've seen the things I most wanted to see, and it's supposed to be nice again tomorrow. So, a day of staying in bed?

Totally fine.

Besides, isn't that what a honeymoon is supposed to be? You're so wrapped up in each other that you hardly see the sights?

Remember, Yvonne, it's not actually a honeymoon.

I tell Leo that we could check out a gallery, if he'd prefer, but he's content to take it easy.

In addition to staying in bed, I spend some time reading in the nook by the window. At four o'clock, we realize we haven't eaten since breakfast. The only things in the room are three bottles of wine and a package of trail mix, and I can't survive on that.

I sigh. "I don't want to leave the room. I don't want to put on pants."

"Yeah, it would be terrible if you had to do that."

I chuckle, then stand up and head to my suitcase, but before I can find some clothes, Leo's arms wrap around me.

"I'll go by myself," he says. "Just tell me what you want to eat."

I could kiss him, and so I do, but I step backward before I can get too distracted. "I'm not picky. Whatever you like."

I read more as he braves the rain. He returns with sandwiches piled high with cheese and prosciutto and arugula, plus tea and a single cookie—for me, of course—and we eat at the small table by the window. The rain has slowed, but it's windy, and yellow leaves dance across our balcony. I've put on pants after all, but only my pajama pants.

After our meal, I open one of the bottles of wine and pour us each a full plastic cup. Since I'm not in the mood to read more, we watch an action movie.

By the time the movie is over, it's only nine o'clock, and the bottle of wine is mostly finished. I wouldn't say I'm drunk, but I'm definitely a little loose from the alcohol. That looseness has me draping myself over Leo and joking about playing strip poker, even though we don't have any cards.

I squeeze his shoulders. "Your muscles are a bit tight. How about I give you a massage?"

He takes off his shirt and lies down on his stomach, on top of the duvet. I remind myself not to get sidetracked as I set my hands on his warm skin. I'm a pretty good masseuse, if I do say so myself, and the noises he makes support that belief. I lose myself in making him feel good, trying to do whatever I can for him.

I don't feel like a people-pleaser with Leo, though. He treats me well, and when we're together, I don't need to censor who I am; I just want to show my appreciation.

Then there are the fantasies that I don't say out loud. It scares me how much I want them.

Another vacation together.

Another naked drawing.

Night after night after night in the same bed.

I think I'm in trouble.

Chapter 25

Leo

I've always liked Yvonne, but two months ago, I liked her just as a pretty woman who was, unfortunately, engaged to my cousin. Sure, I knew that perfect lighting followed her wherever she went, and she seemed kind and thoughtful and better at making small talk than me. But although I was drawn to her, I didn't know her well.

I didn't know what it was like to share a meal with her, just the two of us.

I didn't know what it was like to look after one of her plants.

I didn't know what it was like to kiss her and bury myself deep inside her and fuck her in front of a goddamn mirror.

I didn't know what it was like to travel with her. Or to hold her in my arms while she sleeps...like she's doing right now, after we split a bottle of wine and she gave me a massage.

A day like today? I wouldn't have let myself imagine it.

And now that I know her even better, I can't help wanting more.

When I sketched her earlier—the first time I'd ever given myself permission to put her likeness on the page—she was so comfortable being naked with me. She enjoyed showing off. I didn't have to encourage her, like I might have in the past.

No, she's open with me, and it makes me wonder...

I shouldn't want more. I've already gotten more than I'd ever imagined—I shouldn't want to keep her, but I do. And I might not be the smartest guy, but I think it might be possible.

Yeah, there's still the whole Carl issue, and if she'd like to take it slow and wait for a little before we tell people, that's okay. I know it's not the simplest situation, but we can make it work, no?

She shifts in my arms, her hair tickling my throat, and a bolt of longing hits me.

Yvonne in my bed? I don't want it to be a luxury.

Well, no. It'll always be a bit of a luxury; I don't see how it could be otherwise. But I want it to be a common one. That should seem impossible for a man like me, but I can't help feeling strangely optimistic.

I'd be good to her, dammit. I certainly wouldn't cheat on her and make her doubt her attractiveness, like my asshole of a cousin. But that's the bare minimum, and I want her to have a hell of a lot more than that.

She asked me to come on this trip—does that mean something?

And if it's not meant to be, why does it feel so damn good to hold her? Why can I spend every minute of the day with her—other than that brief trip to get takeout—and still feel like it's not enough?

Yeah, it's midnight, and everything is a bit hazy, but I think I should ask her.

Not tomorrow. It's the last full day of our vacation.

Maybe I'll do it on the drive home.

Chapter 26

Yvonne

WHEN I WAKE UP on Tuesday morning, I don't feel disoriented. This is the third morning I've woken up next to Leo, and I'm starting to get used to it.

That gives me pause.

I don't feel very single right now, not when I keep waking up with a man in my bed. Not when I'm inserting him into my dreams for the future.

"Hey," he murmurs, stroking my hair back from my face.

"Morning." I swallow past the lump in my throat. "It looks like a nice day."

"What do you want to do?"

Because I did extensive research for this trip, I have lots of ideas. After a zucchini and tomato frittata, served with toast and homemade jam, we go to another state park, then head to a cidery for lunch. Our table is on the heated patio, which has a lovely view of the orchards. The patio isn't busy, perhaps because it's a Tuesday, and even with the heaters, it might be slightly chillier than some people would prefer.

While we're waiting for our food, my phone buzzes. It's Tracey, sharing a photo of Isaac. As I show it to Leo, I decide this would be a good time to ask him a question.

"Do you want kids?"

Most people want kids, don't they? Odds are he does, and that will shut down any romantic fantasies in my brain because it's not something I'm willing to compromise on. I know what I want, and I won't change my mind.

He shakes his head. "One of my exes...she had a pregnancy scare and it..." He scrubs a hand over his face. "It scared the shit out of me. I don't usually freak out, but that did it. A few months later, I got a vasectomy."

I choke on my cider. This certainly isn't where I thought the conversation would go. A man so serious about not having kids that he's had a vasectomy by the age of thirty?

A familiar notch appears between his eyebrows. "Is something wrong?"

"No."

That's a lie. It's wrong that I'm imagining our child-free future together. It's wrong that I'm feeling so attached. Maybe I'm only thinking of a future with him because being alone frightens me.

However, there's still some time left in our trip, and I might as well enjoy it. When I smile at Leo, that seems to reassure him, and the notch becomes only a faint line.

And when he takes my hand as we walk across the parking lot after lunch, I don't pull back.

We have a nice dinner together in Ithaca, and when we return to the bed and breakfast, we head to our balcony. A keen sense of sorrow envelops me...but then Leo's arms are around me, his chest against my back, and that stems my melancholy. He's here for now.

He presses kisses up and down my neck, and I turn my head to meet his mouth. I try to etch everything about this moment into my memory. His soft yet needy lips on mine, his hand sliding under the hem of my dress, the night breeze on my face. As I shut my eyes, that hand slides up farther, toying with the elastic band on my underwear...and I hear a door slide open.

I freeze. Leo's mouth stills on my neck.

"Don't mind us," someone says.

I open my eyes. There are no outside lights, only the light that spills out from our room, but I can easily make out a couple on the balcony next to ours, a man and a woman.

"We won't watch," the man says good-naturedly. A big white guy, maybe a few years younger than me.

There's a long, oddly charged moment, and I'm unable to move. My feet feel like they're glued to the balcony.

Then the woman—a petite South Asian woman with a bob—says, "Unless you want us to watch."

She's joking. I think.

Well, she said it as a joke, but as I meet her eyes, I can tell...it's an invitation, if I want it to be. My breath hitches. She winks at me, and I find that wink strangely alluring.

"What do you think?" Leo murmurs in my ear. "You want to give them a little show?"

I can feel everyone looking at me. It's different from watching myself in front of a mirror, but there's something exhilarating about it. I wasn't sure I'd be into this, but...

All of a sudden, my panties are soaked.

When I grip the railing of the balcony and nod, Leo's quiet laughter tickles my skin.

"Show them your tits," he whispers. "You have great tits. They deserve to be admired."

I nod again, and he starts working on the tie at the back of my halter dress. I feel a sizzle of anticipation. He lets the front of my dress fall, exposing my breasts to the night air. My gaze remains on the couple in front of us, bouncing from her face to his.

Who *am* I?

I'm bad. I'm filthy.

I'm powerful.

My nipples are stiff peaks—and it has nothing to do with the cool breeze.

Leo turns me a little, then dips his head and takes one nipple into his mouth. The man across from me hisses, and I thrust my chest toward Leo and squeeze my other breast with my hand.

I whimper. I'm close to coming, and he hasn't even touched me *there*.

He straightens up and rotates me so I'm fully facing the other balcony again. His hand inches up my leg and slips inside my panties.

"You love this, don't you?" he murmurs when he discovers how wet I am.

It's like we're in our own little world, even though we're being watched.

They won't be able to see exactly what Leo is doing between my legs, but they'll be able to see where his hand is...and how it affects me.

I'm a ball of sexual need.

His finger penetrates me, and I bite my bottom lip so I don't cry out and disturb the silence of the trees around us. His other arm is wrapped around me, his hand securely on my breast, and his mouth is on my shoulder. My hands tighten on the railing, and I'm thankful for the boundary between us and them, even as I enjoy their attention.

A part of me is horrified that they can probably hear how wet I am, as Leo moves his finger in and out. But at the same time, it's electric. Every inch of me is buzzing with awareness.

Leo adds a second finger. My mouth drops open, but I manage to stay quiet.

I imagine how I must look: chest exposed, pure need written on my face, a man's hand between my thighs. I was supposed to be on my honeymoon, a good little wife...

"That's right, baby," Leo says. "Ride my hand. Come for me."

I squeeze my eyes shut and open my mouth in a silent scream.

I'm here. Watch me.

When I finally open my eyes, they're gone.

I turn in Leo's arms and look him in the eye for the first time in several minutes. His gaze is hungry and his lips are parted.

"I need to be in you," he growls.

He takes me to bed and tears off my clothes in record time. I'm not sure how it's possible, but he's even more desperate than usual. He crushes his mouth against mine, and his hands feel like they're everywhere all at once.

As he enters me, I hear the headboard in the next room knock against the wall. I smile before clenching Leo's cock.

"*Dammit*," he bites out. "I won't last if you keep..."

He doesn't last long, but he makes sure I come again first. Bliss floods my body, and I feel like I'm top of the world.

Once he pulls out, though, I'm wrung dry, my limbs heavy. He strokes my hair and tells me I'm amazing, and he holds me close for a long, long time.

I've been sleeping well on this trip, but the last night is a different matter. Leo falls asleep right away, but an hour later, I'm still up, even though I'm tired.

It's like my brain doesn't want to sleep when it means I'll miss out on some of the little time I have left with him—and isn't that a silly thought?

He's just a man who helped me get over my engagement. The man who showed me what good sex could be like, both in and out of bed. Who exposed my breasts to complete strangers and made me come in front of an audience.

He's not the love of my life, even if I brought him on a rather romantic trip.

When I think of not seeing him again, every part of me aches. That pain is just proof that when we return to Toronto, I need to stop hanging out with him before I get even more attached. It's what is best for me, and I haven't always done what's best for myself in the past, but I need to focus on that now as I rebuild my life. I've learned things from my time with him, but I have to move on.

I run my hand over his back, as gently as I can so I don't disturb him, and try not to cry.

On our last morning together, I wake up early, even though I didn't fall asleep until three. As the sun begins to brighten the room, I study Leo's sleeping form. He's on his side, turned toward me, and when he opens his eyes, he smiles.

I roll him onto his back, throw my leg over his hips, and kiss him. We don't speak as I rub myself against him, as he slides down my body and licks me until I whisper his name. We don't speak as I roll on the condom and I lower myself onto his cock for the very last time. We simply look at each other, and when that becomes too much, I close my eyes and just let myself enjoy how he takes such pleasure in my body and gives pleasure back to me in return.

When I'm ready to start dating again, I know exactly what I want.

He pulls out of me, presses a kiss to my forehead, and heads to the washroom...and I feel emptier than I've ever felt in my life. A single tear slides down my cheek.

I wipe it away before he returns.

At breakfast, we see the other couple at a table across the room. The woman winks at me, and I smile back before ducking my head. It's weird to see them in the light of the morning, weird to be confronted with evidence that it actually happened and wasn't just a dream.

Despite my slight embarrassment, I don't regret it. I don't regret *him*.

But I have to move on.

I've always been good at pretending. I can do it again.

Chapter 27

Leo

ACCORDING TO GOOGLE MAPS, it'll take about four and a half hours to drive back. Add a few stops—coffee, gas, lunch—and I figure it'll be at least six hours. We'll arrive at my parents' house on the early side of rush hour, if we're lucky.

Yvonne falls asleep as soon as we get on the I-90, which is a relief. I can't ask her anything serious if she's unconscious, and I'm not as hopeful as I was on Monday night. There were moments yesterday when something seemed off, and she tried to paper it over, even though she usually doesn't try to do that with me. But she did hold my hand, and after a hot night together, we had sex again this morning.

She awakens groggily as I'm getting coffee at a Tim Hortons—I didn't know there were any Tim Hortons in the US until this trip. I ask if she wants anything, and she shakes her head before closing her eyes, not opening them until we go through customs. She's conscious only briefly before she shuts her eyes again.

I wonder if she's actually sleeping. Maybe she's avoiding me?

More than an hour later, we hit traffic on the 403. I mutter a curse as I come to a sudden stop.

"Where are we?" Yvonne murmurs.

"Mississauga," I say.

"I can't believe I slept that long."

Hmm. Maybe she really was asleep.

I give it a few minutes, and as we're traveling at the break-neck speed of 20 km/h—certainly no speeding tickets for me today—I figure it's time.

"I was wondering...what happens now." I've had hours to think about what to say, but I've never been good at planning my words in advance.

"What do you mean?" she asks.

"I'd like to keep seeing you—and not just for sex."

"Oh."

This is followed by a very, very long pause. I might not be an expert in communication, but I know nothing good is coming after that. I can practically feel her pasting on a smile.

"I'm very grateful," she says, "for all you've done for me in the past couple of months."

This is the last thing I want. Polite words, like the ones she'd say to my parents. Words I don't even deserve, not when I feel like a selfish ass.

"I didn't fuck you because I was *kind,*" I hiss.

"I'm not just talking about that." She's forcing her voice to be light. "You drove me around after I ran from my wedding. You helped me pick up my stuff. You—"

"—had a crush on you." The word seems insufficient, too childish to describe my feelings, but it's what I say.

"*What?*"

The good thing about driving is that I don't have to look at her. It's not rude to avoid eye contact when you're in front of the wheel; it's safe.

"You hardly knew me then," she protests.

"I didn't say it made sense."

"I was engaged to your cousin."

"Which is why I never mentioned it. I'm not that stupid." I wasn't smart enough to feel otherwise, but I respected that she'd made a choice.

"Don't call yourself stupid."

I don't respond.

"When I asked if you wanted to sleep with me," she says, "you immediately said no."

"I knew it was a bad idea, even though I wanted it. I thought I made that clear."

And I was right. It *was* a bad idea.

It made me believe it was possible to have more, and now I don't have to use my imagination; I can just use my memory. When it comes to Yvonne, the images are even more vivid than usual, particularly the images of last night.

"Since when?" she asks.

"Since always." No point in lying when I've already told her this much.

"You told me that you hadn't had sex in years. Did you—"

"I couldn't interest myself in anyone else." I chuckle without humor. I didn't want it to be that way, but it was.

"Your feelings didn't change when you realized I was actually a bit of a mess? When I forced you to look after Francine?"

"No. They got worse."

She frowns. "I don't understand."

"You think people only like you because you have your shit together, but that's not true. At least, it's not true for me."

She's quiet once more. "I don't think we should see each other at all."

Her words are a punch to the gut, but I try not to show it. I tighten my hands on the steering wheel and look ahead at the never-ending traffic.

"The timing is all wrong," she says. "I just got out of a five-year relationship. I don't have space in my life for this, and even if we weren't calling it a relationship this past week, it was starting to feel like one—that's why we shouldn't see each other at all."

"What if the timing wasn't wrong?"

"And if you weren't Carl's cousin?" She sighs. "I'm sorry."

The tenderness in those words breaks something inside of me, but I merely nod and grip the steering wheel even harder, amazed it hasn't cracked yet. She touches my shoulder.

"Don't," I say, and the word echoes in the car. I rarely raise my voice, and I cringe whenever I do. Now is no exception, but I don't apologize.

I'm not her.

The rest of the drive is tense, to say the least. I'm annoyed with myself for ever thinking I could have the impossible. Why did I have to ask her and make things weird? I should have just enjoyed the days I'd been given; I shouldn't have been greedy.

I think of the sketch. I wonder if she'll ever look at it again, or if it'll be too painful.

But maybe it won't be painful for her. She turned me down, after all. She said the timing was wrong, but maybe that was just her avoiding the truth. If it seemed otherwise, that was just me being foolish and—

"Leo!"

I slam on the brakes a moment later than I should have, but it's enough to avoid hitting the car in front of me.

Finally, traffic starts moving again, thank God. I have no idea why we're suddenly going at a half-decent speed—it's not like we passed any accidents or construction—but I'm glad for it. I can drop Yvonne off at my parents' house as soon as possible and stew alone in my apartment.

We encounter a little traffic again once we're on the 401, but at last, I'm pulling into my parents' driveway.

Then I realize what I've done.

I picked up Yvonne elsewhere. Nobody—aside from Shauna—is supposed to know that I went to the Finger Lakes with her.

My parents shouldn't be home from work for another half hour, though. She'll get her stuff from the trunk and I'll get the hell out of here, and with any luck, no one will notice.

I turn to look at Yvonne, but she's already gotten out of the passenger's seat.

And then I hear a most unwelcome voice.

"I knew it."

Chapter 28

Yvonne

I freeze, halfway out of Leo's car, and look in horror at the familiar mini-SUV that has driven up beside us. It doesn't belong to Howie or Lynne.

No, it's worse than that.

"I *knew* it," Carl says again. He's standing in between the two vehicles as his mother gets out of the driver's side.

Yeah, that's Gladys's SUV.

If only we'd remembered that I wasn't supposed to be dropped off here. If only Leo had let me go a couple of blocks away. But I was in a weird headspace.

If only he hadn't confessed his feelings for me.

That was the last thing I expected. For Leo to say he always liked me and wanted a relationship.

Oh my God.

This feels like the worst mess of my life, even worse than that time I left my fiancé at the altar. But this time, I can't run.

I walk around the car, until I'm a few steps from the man I was supposed to marry. I haven't seen him since that day, and now I wonder how I ever said yes to his proposal.

Who was that woman?

"Knew what?" I say.

"That you left me for him." Carl jabs a finger toward the window of Leo's car, which looks old and shabby compared to the other vehicle in the driveway, but I don't care.

"I didn't."

"Why are you denying it?" Gladys is standing in front of me now. "My husband saw you at IKEA together, and today, Carl's friend saw Leo at a Tim Hortons near Buffalo."

"Which wouldn't be so suspicious," Carl says, "but upstate New York is where we were supposed to go on our honeymoon. You took my cousin on our honeymoon!"

I can't believe this is my life, though at least they don't know about last night.

Ha!

I try to compose myself. "Yes, I did, but—"

Leo opens his car door, and as soon as he steps outside, Carl punches him in the face.

"Leo!" I cry.

I expect him to fight back, but he just slumps against the car. Not confident that Carl won't throw another punch, I stand in between them.

"Your fight is with me, not him," I tell my ex.

"I can't believe I was so wrong about you," Carl mutters.

"You wanted a sweet little stay-at-home mom as a wife, and yeah, I left partly because I realized I didn't want that. Besides, you were a lousy partner who never appreciated anything I did for you. I didn't leave you for him—no, I left for *me*."

"You're not making sense," Gladys says. "Any woman would be lucky to have my son."

"I'm making perfect sense." I turn to Carl. "I was so anxious about the future you had planned out for us, and you wouldn't listen when I tried to talk to you about it. I should have left when you cheated on me."

I look at Gladys and feel a grim sense of satisfaction at the shock on her face, but I'm soon distracted by the Camry driving up the road. Lynne parks on the street because she can't get into her own driveway. Lynne, who has been so generous to me and hates this sort of drama.

But I can't stop.

"You don't believe me?" I say to Gladys. Her mouth is still hanging open. "I have screenshots and everything. I can show you."

I probably shouldn't be trying to convince Carl's mom that he really did cheat. But it's suddenly important to me that she know the truth, even though I expect her to defend him, maybe even say I forced him to be unfaithful. Her precious son.

Leo is still leaning on the car door behind me, and now Lynne has joined the crowd, but she hasn't spoken. It's as tense as that last part of the drive, and my heart is beating furiously.

"I swear I wasn't cheating," I tell Carl. "I hardly knew Leo until he drove me away from the church—and that only happened because he was late to the wedding. You're just projecting. You think that because you were cheating on me, I was cheating on you, too, and it's the only explanation for me running."

It's a relief to speak the words out loud. I'm tired of keeping his dirty secret, especially when he's throwing accusations at me. Even if this makes no difference, I'm glad I did it.

To my shock, Gladys grabs her son by the ear.

"Is it true?" she hisses.

"Ma!" Carl says. "You're hurting me."

"*Is it true?*"

"Yes, but I promised it would never happen again and—"

"Aiyah! I raised you better than this!"

Gladys actually looks disgusted with him. I assumed he could do no wrong in her eyes—and based on Carl's expression, so did he.

I never thought I'd see the day.

She's still tugging on his ear, and he's wincing in pain, his head at an awkward angle—she's a foot shorter than him. I smother my laughter as she shoves him into the SUV.

"I'm sorry for causing such a commotion at your house," Gladys says to Lynne. "Leo, you should put some ice—"

"I can take care of it," Lynne assures her.

They drive away, and now I'm the one who feels the need to apologize.

I turn to Lynne. "I'm so sorry."

"What do you have to be sorry for?" she asks.

"If I'd called off the engagement months ago—"

"You say you're sorry all the time, but Gladys? She never does. At least, she never says it and means it, and you got her to do that. I will never forget." Lynne seems to be doing her best to put a positive spin on this, and I don't feel like arguing.

We both turn to Leo.

"He punched you?" Lynne asks. "Did you at least punch him back?"

Leo merely grunts.

"He did not," I clarify, trying not to chuckle at her disappointment.

Leo, on the other hand, is expressionless. I can't believe I turned him down and got him punched, all in the span of sixty minutes. I don't know how to make it better.

Another car drives up and parks on the driveway next to Leo's car. Howie jumps out. "Are you okay? Someone on Nextdoor said there was a fight at my house!"

Are the neighbors looking out their windows? I don't see anyone else outside.

Lynne takes his arm. "I will explain." She leads him inside, as if wanting to give me and Leo some space.

I exhale when we're alone, then place my hand on his cheek. He flinches.

"Is it really painful?" I ask. "Maybe you should go to the doctor—"

"I'm fine." He takes a step back, and that breaks something inside me.

We've spent so much of the last five days touching each other. It'll take a little while to get used to this, but I know it's for the best. I need to learn who I am by myself. I already stayed longer than I should have with one man; I won't make that mistake again.

I wish I could kiss Leo one last time—I *ache* to kiss him—but instead, I simply say, "Goodbye," and head into the house before I can thank him again.

I know he wouldn't want that.

"Where's Leo?" Howie asks when I enter the kitchen.

"He left." I pause. "Just so you know, we're not actually together, though yes, he did go on the trip with me. I pretended I was going with Shauna because I knew how it would look, but…"

Yup, I slept with your son, and how awkward is this?

Maybe I shouldn't have gone on that honeymoon. Maybe I shouldn't have propositioned Leo. I should have waited until I had my own apartment, then tried to find someone on an app who'd show me what good sex is like, though it's hard to imagine it would have been nearly as enjoyable with anyone else. He made me feel special, more desirable than I've ever felt in my life. The idea that he'd secretly wanted me for two years is a little thrilling, even though I turned down his request for a relationship.

"We're still helping you move tomorrow?" Howie asks.

I'm thankful for the change in topic. "If you can, yes, I'd really appreciate it."

"What else are we going to do?" Lynne says. "We already took the time off."

"You didn't need to—"

She shoots me a quelling look.

I'm about to head upstairs when the doorbell rings.

"Aiyah!" Lynne says. "Now what?"

"I'll get it." Howie places a hand on her shoulder before walking to the front door. I follow him because I can't help thinking that once again, their visitor has to do with *me*.

I'm not wrong, though I certainly wasn't expecting to see my mother on the doorstep. I don't know how she got this address. She looks smaller and slighter than usual.

My heart rate kicks up. "Is something wrong?"

"Can I talk to you? I have Doris's car." She gestures toward the street. "We can sit there."

"Why do you have her car? What happened to yours?"

"Ah, no need to do that." Howie waves my mother inside. "You can sit in the front room. We won't bother you." He turns to me. "If you need anything to eat, help yourself."

Ma and I head to the front room, and I close the French door before taking a seat next to her on the couch.

"What's is it?" I ask. "You're scaring me."

I can't help thinking of Tracey, but Ma doesn't even know where Tracey lives. They don't communicate, except via me, so if something happened to Tracey or Isaac, I would learn first.

"I left," Ma says.

"Left what?"

"Your father."

I stare at her, unable to comprehend her words.

"I know you're shocked," she says. "I never thought I could...but then you ran, and everything turned out okay."

I think of the scene on the driveway, not half an hour ago, and let out an unhinged laugh.

"No?" She frowns. "Do you regret it?"

I shake my head. "Definitely not."

"That's good. Then I'm glad you did it." She pats my arm.

"But you were pissed, even after I told you that he cheated. You said I should have gone through with it."

"I still don't like all the wasted money, but better not to marry than to..." She looks away. "Be like me."

"Ma..."

I never thought my parents had some great love story, but I didn't expect this. What *was* their marriage like? I have a feeling that my sister knew more than I ever did.

As if reading my mind, Ma says, "I didn't want to be so hard on Tracey, but your father wouldn't hear otherwise. Whenever she got a bad mark, he blamed me. He said I was too soft."

"Are you safe?" I ask. "Where are you staying?"

"With Doris."

She's one of my mother's oldest friends, and I'm glad that Ma has her. Still, I feel only a shred of relief.

"Are you safe?" I repeat. My father never laid a hand on me, but that doesn't mean...

She nods.

I blow out a breath. "You're glad you left?"

"Yes." She finally smiles. It's weak, but it's there. "I feel like a huge weight has been lifted off me." She puts her hands on my shoulders. "You were so brave. I don't know how I raised such a brave girl. You and Tracey... You will tell her for me?"

I nod and wait for another request. An actual visit with her grandbaby. Tracey's number. Anything like that.

But none comes.

"I should go," Ma says, "but you'll visit me, yes? It's fine with Doris."

"I will."

Ma gives me a tentative hug. She leaves before I can fully comprehend what happened, and Howie enters the front room.

"Is everything okay?" His usual jovial expression is filled with concern, which I've never seen in my own father's eyes. My father approved when I got good marks and when I got engaged to an acceptable man, but there was never affection, never concern.

"Yes," I say. "Everything is fine."

But later that day, as I prepare for bed, I certainly don't feel fine. There's the move tomorrow...and then there's Leo. I pull out the sketch and look at it for a moment, but then I feel too exposed and put it back.

I hate that my tool of an ex punched him.

I hate that I hurt him, too.

Leo wouldn't have asked for anything more unless he truly meant it. He must be broken-hearted right now, but what else could I do? As I said, I need to take time for myself.

Yet a part of me feels like I made a mistake. Leo isn't like my ex-fiancé—and he isn't like my father. He doesn't have set expectations for how I'm supposed to act or what I'm supposed to accomplish. He just likes me as I am, even when I allow myself to be messy.

I cover my face with my hands as I think of what happened on the driveway earlier.

Everyone *knew*.

I don't like feeling this exposed. Watching Leo fuck me in front of the mirror—and in front of that couple—was a different sort of exposure. I was in control.

I send him a text.

ME: Are you okay?

LEO: I'm fine

Just two words, yet I can't help reading them over and over. Leo can be taciturn at times, and I'm sure they don't tell the whole story.

But I can't demand that he tell me more.

With a sigh, I set down my phone. Tomorrow, I'll have my own little apartment that I can decorate however I like. I should be more excited, but I can't help thinking about the fact that twenty-four hours ago, I was in bed with Leo. So much has happened since.

I'm sure I'll get over him soon, though.

I mean, it's not like we were ever engaged...or even properly dating.

Chapter 29

Leo

I WALK INTO THE office with my head down, hoping I don't look like death warmed over, or whatever the expression is. However, it's hard to conceal my black eye, and Dinesh apparently notices it from across the room.

"So, I have to ask," he says as I pour my coffee. He's got his usual smile, but his brows are creased with worry.

"My cousin punched me in the face," I say simply.

He waits for me to elaborate, but I don't.

"Uh," he says. "Did you punch him back?"

"No. I deserved it."

"Why?"

I'm not in the mood for this.

"Because I slept with his fiancée," I say abruptly, then walk away.

When I reach my desk, I look back. Dinesh's mouth is hanging open. Hmm. Probably should have said "ex-fiancée" so he thinks I'm less of an asshole. Oh well. Maybe he'll stop talking to me, the guy with questionable morals, which seems like a plus right now. I don't want to talk to anyone.

"You okay?" Pablo asks. I'm not sure if he heard that conversation.

"I'm fine," I mumble, and thankfully, Pablo doesn't question my words, the same ones I sent to Yvonne last night.

The truth is, I do feel like I deserved it. Even if Carl is a jackass, it still seems shitty to sleep with his ex soon after the wedding that didn't happen, and to go on the honeymoon with her.

Besides, I had no fight in me. After Yvonne shot me down in the car, I just didn't care anymore. What was the point in fighting back? I deserved that punch for being silly enough to think I could have something real with her. I deserved to have some sense knocked into me.

I rub my eyes and turn on my monitor. The tasks that are usually manageable for me now seem impossible. Coming back to work after a few days off is always hard, but not like this. How the fuck am I supposed to get anything done?

I can't stop thinking of her radiant smile as we walked under the waterfalls at Watkins Glen. Of the sight of her sleeping beside me...sitting across from me at a candlelit table...

After an unproductive morning, I'm eating lunch when I get a text.

> EVAN: Hey. Isobel told me what happened. You okay?

I want to snap at him. If he were here, I probably would, and he'd back away slowly with a smile on his face because he's the nice one.

Isobel is Carl's sister. I'm sure everyone knows by now. Figures.

I tell him that I'm fine. I think I'll be doing that a lot.

What's the alternative? To talk about how I really feel? Telling Yvonne that I want to keep seeing her, that I've liked her from the moment I met her, was enough for the month. Hell, it was enough for the year. I don't want to discuss my feelings anymore.

Another text arrives.

MAX: Should I be worried about you?

Knowing Max, he'll worry no matter how I reply. I say I'm fine, then stab my food with my fork and wonder how Yvonne's move is going.

I also wonder if the only reason she wanted me was the attraction of the forbidden. Her ex's cousin. Probably not the kind of guy her parents would approve of, even if I weren't related to Carl. I called her a bad girl, and she loved it. She got off on it.

I thought there was more to us than that, but I'm good at being wrong.

Chapter 30

Yvonne

Howie, Lynne, and I load the small amount of stuff I brought from my apartment with Carl, as well as some of old furniture that Lynne offered me, into the borrowed truck and set off. A delivery from IKEA will bring everything else.

My new landlord meets me at the building with my keys, and I do my best to give off polite, friendly, I-will-be-the-perfect-tenant vibes.

When I step inside my new apartment, I can't help smiling. It's mine! I don't own it, but it's mine for at least a year. I can do whatever I like with it—within reason, of course.

Back at the truck, Howie reaches for the heaviest box of plants. When I insist on carrying it, he grabs my large suitcase, stuffed with most of my clothes.

"No, you shouldn't," I say. "I'll do it on the next trip."

"We're not that old," Howie protests. "We can manage. The suitcase has wheels."

Hmm. This is true.

Though we struggle a bit more with the bookcase and dresser, it doesn't take too long to get everything into the apartment. The van with my furniture arrives right on time, and I immediately start working on assembly.

"It's okay, you don't have to stay," I tell Lynne and Howie.

"Is Leo coming to help you later?" she asks.

"No."

There's an awkward pause, and they look at each other.

"Aiyah!" Lynne says. "He will go on vacation with you but won't help you move?"

I shut my eyes. "Like I said, we're not together. If I asked him, I'm sure he'd do it"—I don't need Leo getting in trouble with his mom—"but I didn't want to bother him."

They look at each other again.

Lynne puts her hand on a cardboard box. "I'm very good at IKEA furniture. Much better than Howie. I'll help you while he makes a couple of calls, okay?"

Sure enough, she does a great job of following the cryptic wordless images while Howie goes into the hall. He returns a few minutes later and starts taking things out of boxes. Lynne has just finished assembling a third chair when there's a knock on the door.

Weird. Maybe it's a neighbor who saw me moving in?

I head to the door, where I'm met by a pizza delivery person. Uh...

"Ah, there it is," Howie says.

Oh my God! They're so sneaky! I can't even buy food for the people who helped me move because they beat me to it.

After telling them repeatedly that it's unnecessary and I will take them out for dinner later this month, we sit down to eat, then assemble more furniture.

By three o'clock, everything is put together, more or less, and I assure them that I can manage from here. They invite me to Thanksgiving at their place, but I lie and say I have plans.

I want to avoid Leo for the time being.

·❤ · ❤ · ❤ · ❤ · ❤ ·

It's weird living on my own.

Of course, there are lots of people around since I live in a high-rise. My unit is next to the elevator, which I can hear. I can also hear when the person above me takes a shower. People walking in the hallway. Traffic on the street below.

But in my unit, for the first time ever, it's just me. There's nobody else to make a mess, nobody to ask what I'm cooking for dinner.

Slowly, I settle into my new life. I get used to the commute. I get used to eating meals alone. I visit my sister and tell her about our parents. "Thank God," she mutters, before saying I can bring Ma next time. I invite Shauna over and give her all the details about the honeymoon and the fight in the driveway. I have coffee with Mary, my old boss. She says I look way more relaxed than the last time I saw her, which makes sense. I'm no longer planning a wedding while having a private meltdown about my future.

But in the middle of the night, I often can't sleep. Whenever that happens, I find myself missing Leo, wishing he were next to me, even though we only slept in the same bed four times.

I can't help it. I miss those few precious days when I got to see him first thing in the morning. I miss texting him from his old bedroom, and I miss driving around the city together. No matter what I needed, he was always there. It's strange to look back on it, now that I know how he felt about me. When I remember his confession, I experience a thrill of pleasure, but I shouldn't. As I told him, I'm not ready for a relationship.

I read posts by women going through divorces, and it makes me realize how lucky I was with Carl. My ex might be a self-absorbed jerk, but he wasn't abusive. I find myself understanding, more than I ever did before, how people can end up in those relationships. The reasons I avoided it have nothing to do with intelligence; lots of smart women end up in abusive situations.

Carl simply wasn't attentive to my needs, and he believed I'd stay anyway because he thought so highly of himself. I'm sure he lied to me a bunch of times—just like he lied to the other woman—but I don't feel traumatized by my years with him.

I know he'll never ask me to take him back. I'll never get that moment of vindication, that chance to shoot him down to his face.

Perhaps he misses all the things I did for him, but I embarrassed him too much.

The weather gets cooler, and I take Lynne and Howie out for lobster. I arrive at the restaurant half an hour early and give my credit card to the server. At the end of the meal, Lynne and Howie do a little dance of saying I shouldn't have, I should at least let them cover half of it, but ultimately, they allow me to pay for the whole thing and don't sneak money into my wallet.

I avoid asking about Leo, but that night, I barely sleep at all.

Shauna finishes my Halloween costume. She decides to zombify her bridesmaid dress as well, and the Saturday before Halloween, we head to a steampunk bar in the Annex. On the trip there, we see lots of other people in costume—there's a box of Kraft Dinner, two witches on bicycles, plus a weirdly sexy zucchini—and I get a few compliments. I also make a toddler cry.

At the bar, I sip cocktails and find myself looking at a man dressed as Ken (of Barbie fame). He's kinda cute. He has a shaved head and...

I think I only like him because he reminds me of Leo.

Shauna dances with Jack Skellington. She gives him her number—her real number—but I don't dance with anyone. A guy who claims to be dressed as Carmy from *The Bear* offers to buy me a drink, and I decline.

On Halloween, I don my costume yet again—with a little less makeup this time—to go trick-or-treating with Erin and her two girls. The younger one is fascinated by Halloween decorations, and she's particularly enthralled by a severed hand; the older one yells at her to hurry up so they can get more candy.

I'm just glad I don't have to deal with bedtime.

Erin is preoccupied with making sure her kids don't run onto the road or knock over a jack-o-lantern, but she asks me how I'm doing.

"I'm fine," I say.

It's sort of true. I'm happy with my new life, even if I'm up at three in the morning more often than I want to be.

By November, most of the leaves have fallen to the ground. While walking to the bus stop, I pass a house with twenty-nine bags of raked leaves out front. But I don't have a yard to tend to; I just have my houseplants.

They all seem to have done okay with the move. Well, aside from Helen, but after some frantic googling, I think I figured out the problem, and hopefully, she'll improve soon. The cuttings from Francine are almost ready to pot, so I'll do that in the next week or two.

And then I'll have to think about seeing Leo.

One night, I pull out the old phone and examine the naughty pictures he took of me. I recall how good he made me feel, how sexy. I flip to the first video, but it seems wrong to watch that now, and I quickly turn off the phone and put it away.

I don't look at the drawing.

And I don't make an account on a dating or hook-up app.

I do occasionally think of the couple next to us at the bed and breakfast, and I wonder what their regular life is like. What's their story? How did they meet? Do they ever think of me, topless in the night air?

And what else could I do to satisfy my exhibitionist streak? Nothing in front of a big audience...but it's hard to imagine anything at all without Leo. I'd prefer to explore it with him.

Though I try not to count the days, I notice when it's the one-month anniversary of the last time we saw each other, the day we returned from upstate New York.

That night, I can't fall asleep. There's an ache between my legs, and—more troublingly—an ache in my heart. I miss his quiet care and thoughtfulness, the way he saw me differently from how anyone else did.

The pressure in my chest is so awful that I release a sob.

I want to wrap my arms around him and run my tongue along the tattoo that snakes around his bicep. I want to take care of him, and I know he'd take care of me in return. Unlike the relationships I've had in the past, it wouldn't feel one-sided. I can't articulate all the reasons I love him, but...

Yes, I love him.

It's a horrible realization.

The timing was all wrong. I couldn't have said yes...could I?

One evening, I take the bus to Auntie Doris's and visit my mom. Unlike me, she's starting to doubt that leaving was the right thing to do. She ended a marriage of over thirty years, though, and I can understand.

But she doesn't go back.

The following weekend, she visits my apartment. She's unimpressed. She complains that it's too small and I have too many plants.

For a few seconds, I consider how I could make the place look bigger, but when I think of getting rid of a single plant...

No. They make me happy.

I don't need my mother to approve of everything I do. This is *my* life, and I will make what I want of it. I don't care what it looks like from the outside.

When she leaves, I look at the picture of Francine for a long, long time.

On my thirtieth birthday, I feel like doing something lowkey, so I meet Shauna at a pho restaurant. As I toss herbs and bean sprouts into my bowl, I ask how it's going with Jack Skellington.

"His name is Antonio!" she says, laughing.

"He'll always be Skellington to me." I pause. "So, how's it going with Antonio?"

She leans forward. "Really well. He even met my dad."

"But you've only known him for two weeks."

"Yeah, well, that's what happens when you live with your parents. It's fine. Dad likes him. I don't think my dad is very picky anymore—he just wants me to get married, now that I'm old."

We're not that old, but I understand. I used to have very clear ideas about where I'd be at thirty.

"Do you want to get married?" I ask before popping a slice of beef in my mouth.

"One day, but I'm in no rush."

I stay silent as I wonder what Leo wants. He doesn't want kids, but we never talked about other aspects of the future.

Shauna reaches across the table. "What's wrong?"

I shake my head. "I don't want to talk about me. We've been doing that too much lately."

"It's your birthday. Besides, you ran away from your wedding, you went on your honeymoon with your ex's cousin, you got a new apartment, your sister had a baby, your mom left your dad—"

"Yes, thank you for reciting all my drama," I mutter, more irritable than usual.

It's probably the lack of sleep.

"I don't mind if we talk more about your life right now," she says gently. "We're friends. Sometimes one person needs more support than the other."

"After I barely talked to you for years, it doesn't feel right."

"Well, that's not going to happen again, correct?"

I shake my head. Not everyone would be as forgiving as Shauna, and I won't take her for granted.

I used to aspire to be more like Val and Jess, who came from richer families than mine and were always so put together. I haven't heard from them since August, and I wouldn't value any advice they'd give me right now, but Shauna...

"I'm not sleeping," I say at last. "I keep thinking about Leo, and I miss him more than I ever missed Carl. When I ran from my wedding, I only missed knowing what my future would be. I missed the days when I wasn't the center of drama. I never missed *him*."

"Maybe you started getting over Carl before you left him, and maybe you got over him so quickly because he's an asshole."

"But I couldn't say yes to a relationship with Leo, right?" I look down at my noodles. "I needed time. If only..."

If I'd met Leo before Carl, it wouldn't have made a difference. I wouldn't have gone for him. He wasn't my type.

"I wish I'd met him six months from now," I say at last.

"You could have asked him to wait. Told him you needed time to figure things out."

"No, I couldn't expect that of him."

"If you asked and he said no, so be it. But I don't think he would have said no, and it's not like he'd have to wait years. I know you really liked him—"

"I love him," I whisper into my pho.

"Well, maybe you should talk to him again."

"But he's Carl's cousin."

"I think Carl forfeited any right to be mad about that when he cheated on you. Besides, lots of people already know that something was going on."

I cover my face with my hands.

"I understand it's not ideal," she says, "but I wouldn't throw the possibility away just because of that. Over a hundred people watched you run from your own wedding, and you didn't retreat to a remote cabin in the woods. You'll manage. I'll support you."

The woman next to us is scrolling through her phone, but I can tell she's listening. I'd be eavesdropping too, if I were her. Several months ago, I would have been shaking my head at someone with a life like mine—and I don't love it now, but it's worth putting myself out there for Leo, isn't it?

I worry about how his parents would respond, but they could have turned their back on me after the incident in their driveway, and they didn't. They even attempted to pay for the lobster dinner.

"So, what do you think?" Shauna asks.

"I'll consider it," I say. "Really, I will."

After pho, we go elsewhere for dessert. I have the most delicious crème caramel gelato, which Leo wouldn't eat because it would be too sweet for him, but he'd be happy for me to enjoy it.

I imagine being cuddled up together on an average Thursday, Leo spending the night in my apartment. I still want to live alone for at least a year, but that doesn't mean I can't have a relationship. And what I want in a relationship is different from what I wanted six months ago, when I was drowning in wedding planning and clinging to my engagement.

That night, full of pho and gelato and cozy under my new flannel sheets, I sleep better than I have in a long time.

The next weekend, I take the TTC to a little plant store that I've been meaning to visit for ages. I buy a black pot for Leo's snake plant. I also buy a watermelon peperomia for myself because I just can't help it.

I pot Leo's plant on my small, cold balcony to avoid making a mess indoors.

I wonder what he's doing now.

Chapter 31

Leo

You'd think I'd be used to not having Yvonne in my life. From the time I met her to the day of her not-wedding, I only saw her at the occasional family function.

But now that I know how it feels to have her in my arms, her absence is unbearable.

God, I miss her so much.

I'd do anything just to watch her eat too-sweet pancakes or drive her to IKEA, but instead, I have to restrain myself from snarling when people try to talk to me. At home, I spend far too much time staring at the spot where Francine used to sit. I even find myself talking to her. Apparently, I'm pathetic enough to speak to a plant that isn't here.

One Saturday in November, more than a month after that stupid black eye, I go to my parents' house. My brothers and I—as well as Kim—sit in the front room while our parents cook. They refuse to let us help.

"I haven't seen you since Thanksgiving, Kim," Evan says. "How was your trip out west?"

Kim chats about her trip to Whistler, where she visited her brother. Evan asks appropriate questions and laughs at one of her stories, as does Jon. I try to listen, but I don't do a very good job of it.

"So, Leo," Jon says. "What about you? Get any more black eyes?"

For fuck's sake. What's wrong with him? Why won't he just annoy Max, like usual?

"As you can see," I say, "I'm fine."

I'm so tired of saying that. I hope my words didn't sound too...growly.

"Seriously," Jon says, "even I wouldn't hit on a woman who'd just left my cousin at the altar."

"Shut the fuck up." This time, I definitely growl.

"Hey, easy there." He holds up his hands, but he's still smiling, that bastard.

I stalk toward Jon, who's seated on the recliner, and his smile slips. Unfortunately, before I can punch my little brother in the face, Evan jumps up and stands between us, and Max is right behind him.

"Violence never solved anything," Evan says.

"Not true," I say. "It'll solve the problem of Jon not having a black eye."

Right now, that seems like a very big problem. A problem that I can fix, unlike some of the other things in my life. I raise my fist just as my mother walks into the room.

Shit.

"Dinner is ready," she says.

We all head toward the dining room, Jon at the front and me at the rear. Mom doesn't let me enter the dining room, though. She puts a hand on my shoulder when we're in the hallway.

Great. Another person who will ask if I'm okay, but I won't snap at her.

"Yvonne is doing well in her new apartment," she says.

"Good. I'm happy for her."

"You don't sound happy."

I don't reply, just try to move toward the food, but Mom blocks my path.

"Look, I know you're disappointed in me," I say. "No need to tell me."

"Didn't we have that talk before? I'm not disappointed in you."

"I don't mean my job or—"

"Aiyah!" She shakes her head. "I know what you mean. We don't always fall in love with the easiest person. I know that...better than you think."

I'm not sure what she's talking about. "You...what?"

She doesn't explain, just pats my shoulder. "Maybe she'll change her mind once she's had some time."

I wonder if Mom knows something I don't, but I tell myself not to hope. I couldn't survive getting my hopes up and having them dashed. I'm in a bad enough state as it is. I suppose I'm better now than I was a month ago, but that's not saying much.

"Also, please don't scare Kim away with your behavior," she says. "They've only been together a few months, and I don't want her to break up with Max because of his family. It's a sore point for her—families, I mean."

"Fine," I huff, refraining from saying that Jon started it, like I might have done as a kid. I don't need to cause problems in my eldest brother's relationship because I'm not happy with my own life. I'm not Carl; I'm not *that* self-centered.

At least, I try not to be, but maybe I should try harder.

I don't talk much at dinner, but I don't usually talk much in a group anyway, so there's nothing weird about that. I decline dessert, but there's nothing weird about that, either. I try not to be too envious of Max and Kim's relationship.

Back in my car, I send a text to a friend I haven't seen in a while, asking if he wants to meet up next weekend. I need to get out and spend less time moping. I don't usually think of myself as a moper, but yeah, that's what I've been doing lately. Moping because I didn't get the woman of my dreams.

I should move on with my life. Not dating—I can't think about that yet—but actually cooking for myself on the weekends and going to the gym. Stuff like that.

When I enter my apartment building, I still feel a bit keyed up. I ride the elevator to my floor. I'll take a shower, then maybe watch some Netflix or just dick around on my phone.

But when I walk down the hall, I see someone sitting by my door, a plant by her side.

Yvonne.

Chapter 32

Yvonne

It took me forever to work up the courage to see Leo. When I finally did, I followed a delivery person into his building, only to find he wasn't home. How anticlimactic.

Since it was eight on a Sunday night, I figured he was working out...or grocery shopping...or possibly visiting his parents. I considered texting him, but instead, I sat down by his door and waited.

And waited.

I entertained myself by playing a variety of word games on my phone, then by learning everything I possibly could about watermelon peperomia, and then by resting my head on my hand and wondering if I'd made a mistake.

It's been a month. Maybe Leo is on a date. Maybe he's even staying over at someone else's apartment tonight.

I have no right to be angry. I gave him up, after all.

I hear footsteps and turn to the left, my heart speeding up, but it's just Leo's neighbor. She gives me a curious glance before opening her door. I try not to sigh as I wonder how much longer I should wait. Should I text him? I—

"Hey."

I startle and drop my phone.

Leo bends down, picks it up, and hands it to me.

"Where were you?" I ask.

"Dinner with my family." He's carrying a bag, presumably full of food from his parents. There's something a little guarded in his voice. Maybe he's unhappy to see me, or he's not sure why I'm here.

"Can I come in?" I ask.

He nods, and when he unlocks the door, I follow him inside with the snake plant. I slip off my shoes in front of the mirror, recalling the first time I was in his apartment. But unlike then, he's not touching me.

"First of all," I say, "here's the plant I promised you."

"Thanks." He nods again and sets it on the counter.

"Second of all." I take a deep breath. "I didn't fully appreciate everything you did for me. I upended my life, but the weeks that followed weren't all that bad, because of you. You had no expectations of who I was supposed to be, and you drove me around and showed me...lots of things." My cheeks heat. "I learned a lot about myself, thanks to you. I'm glad you got that speeding ticket—I hope it wasn't expensive."

His lips quirk, but otherwise, his expression remains the same.

"I wish I hadn't turned you down," I say. "I'm sorry for hurting you. You might not always show it, but I know you feel things quite a bit. I wish I'd told you that I needed some time to myself first. Now that I've had that time, I want to be with you, if your feelings haven't changed."

A slow smile spreads across his face, and it fills me with warmth. Leo might not be the most cheerful guy, but when he does smile, it's breathtaking.

"They haven't." He steps toward me.

I'm desperate to feel his arms around me, but I hold up a finger. "I need you to be aware of a few things. I'm not sure I ever want to get married, and if I do, I certainly don't want to plan another big wedding. I also want to live by myself for at least year. And, like I told you, I don't want kids."

I feel like I'm making this too much about myself. Perhaps after all the years of focusing on what others want for me, I've swung too far in the other direction.

"I'm flexible on a lot of other things," I tell him. "Just not those, and if this is going to work, I need you to know that from the start."

"I understand. That's fine." He pauses. "I've been saying 'I'm fine' a lot lately, but this time, I really mean it."

I hate the thought of him being in agony. "Leo…"

"I probably shouldn't have told you that I've always had a crush on you. It was too much. True, but too much."

At the time, it did shock me, but… "I'm glad you told me."

I slide my hand up his cheek, and he pulls me close and presses a slow kiss to my lips.

Being together feels so good. So right.

"One more thing," I say. "Early next year, I'd like to take a short vacation with you. A trip that I plan just for us, not a trip that I planned to take with someone else. I'll arrange all the details. Is that okay?"

"Of course. As long as it's with you."

I smile, knowing he really means that. He wants *me*, not some list of traits that he thinks would fit well into his life.

Despite what happened in my last relationship, I feel confident I've made the correct choice. My gut says this is right, and I'm not used to listening to it; I'm used to doing what I think I should do, which wouldn't be dating my ex-fiancé's cousin. But it turns out that I like being a little messy after all.

If I tried listing my reasons to stay with Leo, I'm sure I could come up with a lot more than three—in fact, it would be an endless list—but they all add up to one simple truth.

"I love you," I say.

"I love you, too."

I'm grateful we can say those words to each other now. My heart is full, and I can't help grinning as I tighten my arms around him.

"Actually," he says, "I have a question for you as well."

"I thought you were a man of action," I tease, sliding my hand under the hem of his shirt. God, I missed touching his warm skin.

"I'll fuck you soon, don't you worry," he murmurs, and that's enough to make me squeeze my thighs together. "But first, I want to know my snake plant's name."

"Your plant's...name?" It's hard to make sense of words when I'm touching him.

"Yes," he says solemnly. "I assume it needs a name?"

I appreciate that this plant is serious business to him. "It's yours. You can name it."

"No. You're the expert."

"Later," I say, and that seems to be the magic word.

He scoops me up and carries me to bed.

Yes, after all this time, I'm *finally* in his bed, and I can't wait to spend lots of time here.

Yvonne's Search History

- winter getaways Ontario

- affordable winter getaways Ontario

- cozy date ideas

- apartment decorating ideas

- unique indoor planters

- light requirements for string of hearts

- plant tattoos

Epilogue

Leo

"Would you like to hold him?" Tracey asks.

I've never held a baby before, but at four months, Yvonne's nephew isn't as small and breakable as he looked in some of the pictures, so maybe it'll be all right.

"Okay," I say.

It's Christmas Eve, and Yvonne and I are visiting her sister for a small holiday get-together. Her mother is also here. It's not the first time that Tracey and her mother have seen each other this year, but I think it's only the second, and the atmosphere is, admittedly, a little strained. Rob is in the kitchen, carving a turkey, and the rest of us are gathered in the living room.

Tracey passes me the baby, who has more hair than I do. I feel a bit awkward holding him, but he gurgles and slaps a tiny hand against my face.

"Ah, you look so tense," Yvonne's mom says.

My girlfriend sighs. "Ma, leave him alone. They're getting along just fine."

"Is that true?" I whisper to Isaac.

He stays quiet, and that's okay. I understand not wanting to talk.

Yvonne's mother doesn't seem to be my biggest fan. She hasn't said as much, but I sense that she doesn't think I'm good enough for her daughter, and...okay, I can understand.

It's still hard to believe this is my life, but if Yvonne thinks I'm the right man for her, I trust her judgment and will do everything in my power to treat her well. I'm glad it's not just sex—though there's a lot of that, too. These days, we make good use of my bed whenever she's over. Sure, we occasionally screw in other places, but afterward, we always find our way to a soft surface so I can hold her close.

Isaac starts fussing, and Tracey immediately takes him back, which is good because I have no idea what to do with a crying baby.

After turkey dinner and presents, Yvonne and I head back to my apartment. We usually spend two or three nights a week together, but we'll be spending more time in each other's company over the holidays. We're both off until January, and we're going to ring in the new year at a party that Shauna's boyfriend is hosting.

Once we're under the covers, I take a small present out of my beside table. Unlike Yvonne, I don't have a Christmas tree in my apartment.

Her face lights up. "Can I open it now?"

When I nod, she slides off the ribbon and tears open the holly-and-ivy wrapping paper to reveal a small box. She lifts the lid.

"Oh my God!" she says. "I love it."

It's nothing expensive, just an enamel keychain of a snake plant. I bought it online from the artist. On the back it says...

"Plant lady!" She laughs, delighted. "It looks just like Vivian."

Vivian is what she named my snake plant, for reasons that are unclear to me, but I take very good care of my only plant, carefully following the schedule that Yvonne set out. I even speak to her on Wednesdays, just like the schedule says, although I suspect that part was a joke.

"You're very sweet, you know?" She presses a kiss to my lips.

"I hate sweets," I mutter.

But yeah, she knows my secret.

"Merry Christmas, Leo," she murmurs, pulling me close.

This is the first time I've brought a partner to my parents' house for Christmas Day, but Yvonne already feels like she belongs. Chinese New Year might be more complicated because we usually do that with our extended family. I don't think Carl is interested in seeing me and Yvonne, even if he has a new girlfriend, but I'm willing to miss the big group event if needed.

Today, though, it's just eight of us. While everyone is enjoying some combination of pecan pie, chocolate truffles, and gingerbread—I skip the pie because it's far too sugary for me—I set my hand on Yvonne's knee under the table. We've been here for several hours already, and I'm looking forward to having her alone.

But then something happens that temporarily wipes such thoughts from my mind.

Evan sets down his fork in a rather decisive manner. "I have some news."

"Oh?" Dad says. "What is it?"

Evan swallows, looking oddly nervous. "I'm getting married."

Jon starts laughing. "Yeah, that's a funny one."

I shove his shoulder to shut him up. Evan wouldn't joke about this sort of thing, although it's been a while since he mentioned dating someone. Unlike me and Max, he hasn't brought anyone to our family Christmas celebration.

So, while congratulations should be in order, most of us are speechless.

Finally, Mom says, "*Who* are you marrying?"

Evan hesitates. "Remember Jane, my friend from university? We've been seeing each other since the summer. I don't usually keep my relationships a secret, but after so many of them ended badly…"

I'm glad this one is different.

But as people get up to hug him and ask questions about the big day, I can't help feeling like he's not telling the whole truth.

What exactly is my brother hiding from us?

About the Author

Jackie Lau decided she wanted to be a writer when she was in grade two, sometime between writing "The Heart That Got Lost" and "The Land of Shapes." She later studied engineering and worked as a geophysicist before turning to writing romance novels. Jackie lives in Toronto with her husband, and despite living in Canada her whole life, she hates winter. When she's not writing, she enjoys gelato, gourmet donuts, cooking, hiking, and reading on the balcony when it's raining.

To learn more and sign up for her newsletter,
visit jackielaubooks.com.

Also by Jackie Lau

Love, Lies, and Cherry Pie

Donut Fall in Love Series
Donut Fall in Love
The Stand-Up Groomsman

Weddings with the Moks Series
Four Weddings to Fall in Love
Three Reasons to Run

Chu's Restaurant Series
The Sitcom Star
The Reluctant Heartthrob

Kwan Sisters/Fong Brothers Series
Grumpy Fake Boyfriend
Mr. Hotshot CEO
Pregnant by the Playboy
Bidding for the Bachelor

Cider Bar Sisters Series
Her Big City Neighbor
His Grumpy Childhood Friend
Her Pretend Christmas Date (novella)
The Professor Next Door
Her Favorite Rebound
Her Unexpected Roommate

Holidays with the Wongs Series
A Match Made for Thanksgiving
A Second Chance Road Trip for Christmas
A Fake Girlfriend for Chinese New Year
A Big Surprise for Valentine's Day

Baldwin Village Series
One Bed for Christmas (prequel novella)
The Ultimate Pi Day Party
Ice Cream Lover
Man vs. Durian

Chin-Williams Series
Not Another Family Wedding
He's Not My Boyfriend

www.ingramcontent.com/pod-product-compliance
Lightning Source LLC
Chambersburg PA
CBHW032252310726
48973CB00008B/2385